"There he is. He done kilt Blake. Don't let him git away!"

Slocum swung around. The other road agents were already after him. He bent over and retrieved the fallen rifle. He pulled back the hammer and aimed. He fired until the magazine was empty. He dropped the rifle and ran to his horse.

Bullets sang past him from four different weapons. The gangs Slocum had heard of in the territory just didn't scare. They were all cold-blooded killers.

Men like these didn't scare—and they didn't forgive and forget . . . .

OTHER BOOKS BY JAKE LOGAN

JAKE LOGAN

SLOCUM AND THE DEADWOOD TREASURE

B

BERKLEY BOOKS, NEW YORK

SLOCUM AND THE DEADWOOD TREASURE

A Berkley Book / published by arrangement with
the author

PRINTING HISTORY
Berkley edition / June 1991

ISBN: 0-425-12843-1

A BERKLEY BOOK ® TM 757,375
Berkley Books are published by The Berkley Publishing Group,
200 Madison Avenue, New York, New York 10016.
The name "BERKLEY" and the "B" logo
are trademarks belonging to Berkley Publishing Corporation.

PRINTED IN THE UNITED STATES OF AMERICA

10 9 8 7 6 5 4 3 2 1

1

John Slocum steadied the long, collapsing telescope on a
rock as he studied the ragged, barren land stretching to the
north. Dakota Territory in September carried more than a
hint of the vicious winter storms that would come roaring
down from Canada, but Slocum hardly noticed. The puffs
of dust rising in the distance held his attention.

He smiled crookedly when he saw the dust clouds near
the rutted road die down. A strong wind whipped through
a narrow ravine in that direction and quickly dissipated the
traces of the masked riders. Slocum turned his telescope
slightly and trained it again on the lumbering stagecoach
making its way to Cheyenne from Deadwood. The huge
wagon was drawn by a team of six horses, already tired
from fighting the steep, uneven trail. The road agents lying
in wait for the stage would find easy pickings.

Slocum followed the stagecoach until it reached the rocky
draw where the highwaymen waited. He saw the blue-black
smoke from their pistols long before the sharp reports
echoed up to him on the low hill. The details of the robbery
were mostly hidden by the undulating terrain, but Slocum
could easily imagine the scenario. Two of the road agents
would stay high on the rocks alongside the road, covering
the driver and the shotgun-toting guard in the box with

well-aimed rifles. The other two or three robbers would get the passengers out and search them for valuables. Then would come the demand for the strongbox.

Slocum found himself breathing faster at the thought. The strongbox must contain enough gold to keep a man happy for a year. The reports of the gold strikes in the Black Hills were nothing short of fabulous—and what did they do with their gold?

It was shipped from the mines and smelters to Cheyenne where it would be safe. Getting it there was the weakest link in the golden chain, and it was here that Slocum wanted to begin sawing away.

He watched carefully and saw how professional the gang robbing the stagecoach was. Rumors of more than ten such gangs working the Cut-Off Trail had reached him over in Fargo. He would have competition for the riches being transported. And he dared not think the pickings would be easy on any of the shipments.

Renewed gunfire snapped him out of his daydream of wealth. This should not be happening. Slocum peered into the eyepiece and watched in amazement as the sides of the stagecoach seemed to fall apart and sprout dozens of rifles. The fusillade of lead tore the road agents to bloody ribbons. Slocum jerked the telescope around and saw that the driver and guard had dropped down into the box, protecting themselves from the riflemen posted on the rocks. The way the bullets bounced off the driver's box, it had to be lined with steel plate, making it about the safest place between Deadwood and Cheyenne.

The gunfire increased. Men poured from the stagecoach, six-shooters and rifles blazing. Slocum saw long tongues of flame reach up toward the highwaymen on the rocks. Bits of rock chipped away as the bullets tore their paths. One road agent jerked and fell forward, dead before he hit the ground twenty feet below. The other slid down the far side of the boulder where he'd made his stand.

Slocum saw the robber wasn't going to escape. The men from the bogus stagecoach circled the boulder in both directions, catching the fleeing robber in a withering cross fire.

Buzzards would have to spit out lead when they ate that carcass, Slocum decided.

He turned back to the coach and studied it, trying to find how it differed from the usual wagon making the Deadwood to Cheyenne run. He couldn't see much difference—and it had probably been built that way. Instead of passengers and hundreds of pounds of gold, it had carried only steel plating and six sheriff's deputies intent on making it open season on road agents.

The men from the coach prowled around, poking here and there, hunting for any robber they might have missed. When they were satisfied, they all got back into the stagecoach. The driver and guard settled down in their seats again, and the stage rattled off. They hadn't even bothered to bury the highwaymen they'd just slain.

Slocum heaved a deep sigh. If men were clever and brave enough to mine gold from the Black Hills, they were also determined enough to see that others, like him, didn't steal their hard-earned treasure. Heaving himself to his feet, he collapsed the telescope tube and put the device away in its canvas bag. He had won the brass and glass wonder in Fargo from a paddle-wheeler captain who was down on his luck. The riverman sailed the Red River from Fargo north to Hudson Bay. Slocum hoped the captain's navigation was better than his skill at seven card stud. The game hadn't lasted an hour before the riverman was tapped out and the telescope was Slocum's.

It was good to be able to reconnoiter before attacking. Slocum had learned that during the war. He stared at the telescope and wondered if it might be possible to connect such a fine sighting device with a sniper's rifle. To be able to hit a target farther away than even his keen green eyes could see unaided would be a potent weapon.

A hint of wind tugged at his brown canvas duster and pulled it back from his six-foot frame. He turned to face the bleak wind and caught the faint sound of hoofbeats challenging the icy blast. Slocum squinted when he saw new dust clouds rising from the dry land. The road agents were long dead and the bogus stagecoach had rolled on, hunting other incautious bands of thieves. He didn't want to tangle with either the law or the Cheyenne and Sioux still roaming the Black Hills some two years after defeating the yellow-haired General George Armstrong Custer over on the Little Big Horn River.

Slocum climbed into the saddle and looked over his shoulder. The riders—at least four from the look of their dust—still rode toward him. Slocum patted the sorrel's neck and said, "Come on, old girl. We've got a ways to go if we want to get out of their path." He took one last look at the riders and added, "Whoever the hell they are."

The horse exploded like a coiled spring and raced down the hill. Slocum was surrounded by tall, dry grass. It didn't give much in the way of fodder for an animal, and it was sere to the point of being dead this late in the year. Come spring the entire plains would turn into a sea of green. But not now. Now there was only the hint of winter and death.

Riding at an angle to the riders' approach, Slocum thought to get out of their way and let them go past. After a half hour's hard ride, he settled down for a mite of a rest near a tiny stream carrying more mud than water.

His sorrel neighed loudly when he dropped to one knee to sample the water. Slocum's gut tightened and his hand went from the impure water to the ebony-handled Colt Navy slung in a cross-draw holster at his left side.

"Don't go tryin' nothing you'll regret, son," came the cold words from behind him. Slocum saw the man's outline reflected in the sluggishly flowing stream. He cursed himself for being so careless. He had concentrated only on the riders. There were dozens of desperate men roaming the Dakota Territory.

"I'm no threat to you," said Slocum. "I'm not a lawman."

"So what makes you think that's a concern, son? Ever enter your mind *I* might be totin' a badge and have come for you? Now tell me. Who 'n the hell are you?"

The words chilled Slocum more than the autumn wind ever could. He had more than one wanted poster circulating in the West. Just after the war he had gone home to Calhoun, Georgia, and found his parents dead—and a carpetbagger judge who had a hankering for the Slocum family land. The no-account judge and his hired gunman were left dead and Slocum never looked back—except when some bounty hunter got too close.

And that was only one warrant. The law hated men who killed judges, even Reconstruction judges, but Slocum had also done his share of robbing to get from Georgia to the Dakota Territory. Any of the warrants would be good enough for a few hundred dollars in reward money.

Slocum estimated his chances. He could draw and fire like lightning, but the man behind him already had a rifle leveled. That much showed in the stream.

"You're no lawman," Slocum said.

"What makes you think that?" The voice carried a hint of amusement. This buoyed Slocum. He had been right. The man who had the drop on him wasn't the law.

"If you were a sheriff, you'd've just shot me in the back. Never seen a sheriff who had an ounce of courage in him."

"Might be a federal marshal. Ever consider that?"

"I've met my share of marshals," Slocum allowed, "and they are usually a damn sight braver than a local sheriff."

"So?"

Slocum had tugged lightly on his horse's reins and gotten the horse to shift its weight slightly in the direction of the gentle pull. It wasn't much, but it was all the chance he had.

"So, marshals tend to be smarter than you." Slocum dived to the side, using the horse as a partial shield. The rifle bullet ripped past his ear and caused a tiny fountain in the stream. Then his Colt was out and blazing away. His first shot found a target in the man's gut.

The man was so thin he hardly cast a shadow. The Winchester he carried dropped from his nerveless fingers to the ground. He followed it, dead before he hit the dirt.

Slocum rolled to his feet and soothed his horse. He didn't like this. He doubted the man was traveling alone. Worse, the riders he had been dodging couldn't be that far off.

The gunshot would draw them like buzzards to a day-old carcass.

He had to satisfy his curiosity first. Slocum knelt beside the man, opened his coat, and exposed his chest, hunting for a badge. He didn't find one. He fingered the fabric of the man's threadbare vest, looking for holes where a star might have been pinned. Nothing. Slocum dug further, pulling out the man's pockets and spilling the contents onto the ground. He found four different penknives, a small pouch of gold dust, and three dollars in greenbacks.

He stood and stared down at his victim. Whoever he had been, he wasn't a lawman. Slocum slipped his Colt Navy into its soft leather holster and guessed he had just cut down a road agent. The four knives hinted that more than one stagecoach passenger had been robbed, and the paucity of gold dust told that the robber wasn't very successful at his chosen profession.

"Let's get on out of here," Slocum said to his horse. Straining, he thought he heard the sound of other horses' hooves pounding. It might have only been his imagination, but Slocum wasn't going to chance it. He had been aimlessly drifting for some time. The rumors of golden riches in the territory were enough to keep him around for a little while longer—at least until he had taken some of those nuggets for his own.

Mounted, he saw that his retreat had been cut off. Two men pulled at their sheathed rifles. As long as they were on horseback, Slocum didn't worry much about them. No one could fire accurately from even the steadiest horse. He had worked long hours with his sorrel and she still shied after the first shot. What did concern him was the positioning of the other men. They had ridden up on either side of the rocky draw and had a good line of fire on him.

Slocum wheeled his horse and started in the other direction. A solitary rider waited for him there. Slocum knew the odds were against him, but in this direction lay his best chance. He spurred his horse's flanks and tore down on the man blocking his escape.

The man drew his rifle from a fancy hand-tooled leather

scabbard and lifted it to his shoulder, easy-like. Slocum knew he was facing a cool customer, one able to knock him out of the saddle with the first shot. If he did that, it wouldn't matter if his horse reared. Slocum would be as dead as the other bushwhacker back at the stream.

Slocum yanked out his six-shooter and blazed away. He didn't care if he hit anything. At this range, hitting the man would have been more a matter of luck than skill. All Slocum wanted was to spook his horse and make his aim just a tad more unreliable.

It worked.

The first slug echoing down the ravine missed Slocum by a country mile. The second went into the air as the man struggled to control his horse. Slocum's minor victory would be short-lived, however, if he didn't get within pistol range.

He rode down hard on the man, closing the distance between them. Slocum lifted his pistol and fired, only to have the hammer fall on an empty chamber. He didn't have time for self-recrimination. When he traveled, he always kept the hammer resting on an empty cylinder, just for the sake of safety. He had already expended the remaining five rounds, one into the bushwhacker and the other four in the wild firing to get the other man's horse to buck.

Slocum shoved the Colt Navy back into his holster and kept riding. It was about the most foolhardy thing he had ever done. He saw the rifle's muzzle as plain as day. It looked big enough to ride into. He imagined he saw the blunt head of the leaden bullet in its firing chamber, waiting for the hammer fall that would ignite the powder and send it tearing into his flesh.

He rode even faster, spurring his horse mercilessly. When he was close enough, he launched himself like an eagle hunting a rabbit. Slocum sailed through the air, his arms wrapping around the rifleman's shoulders. A heavy impact on the side of his head told him the man had swung the rifle at the last instant, using it as a club.

Slocum and the rifleman tumbled to the ground. Slocum was ready for the fall. The other man wasn't. He had the air knocked from his lungs and lay gasping like a fish out of water.

Sheathed at the small of his back, Slocum always carried a thick-bladed hunting knife. It slipped free now and drove down hard into the other man's belly.

The man looked up, his expression unreadable. Then he died.

Slocum rocked back, resting on his knees and staring at the man. He had killed twice within minutes. Both times had been in self-defense. Searching this man's chest for any sign of a badge proved futile, also. Whoever Slocum had come up against, it wasn't the law.

In its way, that might be even worse than running afoul of some small-town sheriff. He would have every outlaw in the Dakota Territory after him and hot for his blood.

"There he is. He done kilt Blake. Don't let him git away!"

The cry from down the rocky draw brought Slocum around. He didn't have the luxury of taking his time. The other road agents were already after him. His hand touched the ebony handle of his six-shooter; then he remembered it was empty. He bent over and retrieved the fallen rifle. He pulled back the hammer and aimed.

The first shot missed, but it caused a ruckus from the five men coming after him.

"Dammit, he's gonna plug us if we keep on," complained one.

Slocum used him as a target. He didn't get a killing shot, but his slug produced a long, loud squall of pain. Slocum fired until the magazine was empty. He dropped the rifle and ran to his horse. The outlaws—and he had no doubt that's what they were—might have let him go if he'd had a few ounces of gold to give them.

Then again, Slocum doubted it. This was a lawless land. Never leave a witness behind. Even if he had enough money to sate their unquenchable desire for riches, they would certainly kill him now. He had cut down two of their number. Somehow he had blundered into their rendezvous. They might think he was a federal marshal come for them, or it might not matter to them. He had to die, no matter what.

Slocum pulled his own rifle and sighted carefully. He missed the rider and got the horse. It was an even better shot than he could have hoped for. The horse collapsed, a bullet through its massive chest. As it fell, it twisted and blocked the trail for the horses behind.

Bullets sang past him from four different weapons. Slocum wasn't going to stand and shoot it out. He just wanted to get away as fast as he could ride. If he was going to do any robbing of his own, he had to stay alive for a spell longer. The narrow ravine turned slightly, going back toward the rocky road where he had seen the bogus stagecoach laden with lawmen.

Slocum kept his heels working at the sorrel's flanks until the horse was flecked with foam. Only when he got to the road did he give the horse a chance to cool off by slowing to a quick walk. Slocum kept looking over his shoulder, expecting to see his pursuers. They never appeared. He doubted he had scared them off. The gangs he had heard of in the territory just didn't scare. Charley Price, Frank Toll, Big-Nosed George, all were cold-blooded killers. Over in Fargo Slocum had even heard that one band was led by a man calling himself McDonald. Rumors had it this was none other than Frank James.

Men like these didn't scare—and they didn't forgive and forget.

He spurred his horse on along the Cut-Off Trail going through Red Canyon. The sooner he got to Custer City the better he would like it. He needed time to get his thoughts together and find out what he was really up against.

2

Slocum pulled his canvas duster tight around him as he rode into the teeth of the wind. It was hardly into September and already he tasted winter in the sharp air slashing at his face and body. But there was something else chilling him. Occasionally he looked over his shoulder, just to be sure. He didn't think the road agents had pursued him. Having left two of their gang dead and at least one other wounded might have infuriated them, but they didn't have the appearance of men ready for a drawn-out fight.

As he rode, he thought about them. He had inadvertently blundered onto some gang's rendezvous. That was the only thing that made any sense. The one who had gotten the drop on him had seemed amused when he had intimated to Slocum that he was a lawman. Only someone running from a dozen wanted posters joked like that.

Slocum pushed it from his mind. He had illicit work of his own to do. The men behind him were competitors for the mountains of gold rolling daily out of the Black Hills mines. Pulling down his battered hat, he gritted his teeth and kept his horse moving forward into the canyon. He wanted to get to Custer City before it got much darker. These weren't hills to be in when you were a stranger.

Shadows lengthened and made the wind seem even

11

colder. Slocum reined in at the mouth of Red Canyon and had to smile at a crudely built wooden sign. Some miner had preceded him along the Cut-Off Trail and had posted: Abandon Hope All Ye Who Enter Here.

Slocum peered into the shadowy hills and saw not despair but dreams. Dotting the hillsides were petered out mines— lots of them. Slocum didn't even bother trying to count the shafts that had given up their wealth to eager miners. That quartz ore had to go into Custer City and Deadwood for smelting. And from there the gold was being shipped three hundred miles to Cheyenne.

Or less, if Slocum was clever enough to hit the right shipment. He looked forward to robbing a stagecoach creaking under the gold's weight and then hightailing it out of Dakota Territory a richer man.

He urged his tired horse forward, keeping an eye out for ambush. He hadn't ridden two miles when he reined in and just stared. Alongside the trail were a dozen poorly marked graves. Two had wooden crosses shoved into the hard, rocky soil. The rest had markers scratched onto rock and nothing more. He stood in his stirrups and craned his neck for a better look. The poorly defined boundaries of the cemetery stretched back down a branching canyon.

Slocum shivered. He knew there were more than simple miners buried here. Gunmen had died here. And innocents. Always the innocent victims perished.

Slocum took the chance to rest and be sure his Colt Navy was reloaded. This time he made sure there were bullets in all six cylinders. The risk of accidental discharge on the trail was outweighed by the need for additional firepower. Just to be sure, he chambered as many rounds as his Winchester would hold and checked the spare Colt in his bedroll.

He was loaded for bear, but he saw nothing living in Red Canyon. Slocum frowned. That hadn't struck him before. It was near twilight. Small animals should be emerging from their daytime burrows to forage for their meager dinners. He saw nothing moving. Nothing. Glancing aloft, he caught sight of a solitary turkey buzzard wheeling on the late afternoon air currents.

Slocum pulled the leather thong off his six-shooter's hammer. He wanted to be ready for anything.

His horse neighed, startling him. He jumped, then forced himself to calm down. He patted the sorrel's nose and led her forward, reins resting lightly in his left hand. Now and then he knelt and checked the trail. No one had passed this way in some time. More than hope had been abandoned along Red Canyon.

He stayed on foot, even though he knew he could make better time riding. Custer City wasn't too far off. Not more than a pair of hours on horseback. Slocum wanted to be sure he got there. Along with the wind whistling through the canyon came a feeling of being watched. Slocum never denied this sixth sense. It had kept him alive through the war and after.

When his horse reared, Slocum tugged hard at the reins. He dropped to one knee and drew his six-shooter. The horse tried to bolt, but Slocum kept her under control. In the dim twilight the horse had seen what it took him several seconds to make out. The trail ahead was littered with bodies.

Slocum advanced, heart racing. The deathly silence wore on him more than if he had been fired upon. He stopped next to the first body, a miner lying facedown on the ground. A Sioux war lance stuck out of the man's back. Slocum didn't have to check further to know the man had been scalped. He walked past and found another miner with three arrows embedded in his back.

The others were similarly slaughtered. The Sioux had lain in wait, let the small party ride past, then had cut them down with arrows until the others in the party had noticed. Only then had the Indians opened up with their rifles. Slocum poked a few of the bodies, but they had been thoroughly stripped of anything of value. No rifles or sidearms remained. He snorted in disgust. If the miners had been toting gold in to Custer City, it was gone, too.

"Damned Sioux," he grumbled. The Indians didn't even value gold. He had spoken with more than one Oglala and Brulé who had expressed confusion over the white man's preoccupation with the metal. They knew the gold was highly valued; after Custer had discovered gold on French's Creek, that much was obvious. The Sioux just didn't know why the gold was so important.

Slocum wondered if it was worth his own life. He had seen the fierce competition to steal—and to keep—the golden treasure. He shrugged it off. It never paid to think too much about such things. If he hit it rich, fine. If not, he would be able to move on and try again somewhere else.

He mounted and picked his way slowly through the field of death. As he rode, he thought about the Sioux, the road agents, and the fake stage carrying the posse. The odds didn't look good for him getting so much as an ounce of that gold, but he wasn't giving up.

He stopped and peered down each canyon branching away from the Cut-Off Trail. Only when he didn't see any movement did he continue. Slocum didn't cotton to the notion of Sioux lying in ambush, waiting for him to pass, and then shooting him in the back as they had done the miners. It was one thing being killed facing your enemy. It was something else to get cut down and never know it. When he died, it was going to be with his six-shooter blazing away.

For an instant, he thought he had imagined the sound of a pistol firing. He shook himself out of his reverie enough to turn and home in on the gunfire. It came from up the canyon to his right. Carried along with the gunfire were wild whoops. War whoops. Sioux raiding party cries.

Slocum knew he would be safer riding straight on along the trail and not turning in the direction of the ruckus. More gunshots echoed down the crossing canyon. The Sioux war party that had massacred the men back on the trail was still prowling and, from the sound of the activity, had cornered more hapless miners.

Slocum decided that anyone in these hills knew what to expect and it wasn't any business of his getting a war lance shoved between his shoulder blades. Custer City was only a couple of hours away. He started to put the spurs to his sorrel when he heard the scream.

A woman's cry for help drifted on the night air and haunted him. He couldn't ride off and let a woman be taken by the Sioux. Against his better judgment, Slocum turned his horse and started toward the fight. He damned himself for a fool. The woman might have been dying when she let out that wail. And where were her menfolk? It was nothing less than criminal to bring a woman out here. Even a place like Custer City was hardly fit for a decent woman.

Slocum dismounted when he heard the clatter of ponies' hooves on rock. The Sioux war party was less than a hundred yards ahead of him. He tethered his sorrel and drew his Winchester from its saddle sheath. He was ready to take on the entire Sioux nation.

Still damning himself for a fool, he advanced. Slocum dropped to his belly when he saw three braves at the foot of a huge mound of tailings from a mine halfway up a hill. The darkness kept him from seeing who defended the mine shaft. The foot-long gouts of flame leaping from the muzzle of a rifle told him someone was still alive.

Slocum raised the rifle and prepared himself to shoot the Indians in the back just as they had done to the miners along the Cut-Off Trail. He never got the chance. One sighted him and all hell broke loose.

Slocum found himself firing steadily at the three braves. He winged one. The other two dived for cover, whooping and hollering for the others in their war party. Slocum didn't stay in one place too long. The muzzle flash from his rifle gave him away as surely as it did the mine's defender up the hillside. Moving quickly and quietly, Slocum flanked the three braves still intending to ambush the occupants of the mine. He barely got the chance to lift his rifle when arms stronger than steel bands closed around his body, pinning his hands to his sides.

He ducked forward and turned. The Sioux brave somersaulted over his back and landed hard at Slocum's feet. Quicker than thought, Slocum whipped out his six-shooter and fired point-blank. The brave jerked and died in one spastic twitch.

The three he had stalked came alive. The one he had wounded limped heavily. Slocum didn't bother finishing him yet. The other two were unscathed and more dangerous—or so he thought. Four quick shots ended their lives.

And Slocum found himself struggling in hand-to-hand combat with the wounded brave. A knife snicked from a hidden sheath and raked across Slocum's face, seeking his throat. He turned slightly and let the ugly gash on his cheek bleed. He could tend it later—if there would be a later for him. He had thought the Sioux warrior too badly wounded to fight effectively. He was wrong. Slocum thought he had tangled with a healthy wildcat.

Slocum grabbed a handful of greasy black hair and used this to turn the Sioux's head to one side. Together they rolled and rolled and rolled until they fetched up hard against a large boulder. Slocum had only one chance and he took it. He slammed the Indian's head against the rock. The Sioux's knife hand opened slightly as the impact jarred the brave's brains.

Releasing his grip on the Sioux's head, Slocum grabbed the brawny wrist with both his hands and twisted hard. Bones snapped and the knife dropped from nerveless fingers. Only then did Slocum finish off the Indian using his own knife.

Panting harshly, Slocum turned away and simply sat, trying to regain his breath. He had been incredibly lucky taking the Sioux braves by surprise. Triumphing over one was a day's work. He had just killed four. And from the sound of the gunfire, he had a way to go before he could rest up.

He took the time to reload and search the four braves for weapons. They all carried knives and bows and arrows. Slocum had tried to use a bow once and found he couldn't hit the broad side of a barn, even if he were locked inside it. He had hoped to use some of the Indians' own ammunition against their comrades, but none had a firearm. Keeping low, he retraced his steps to where he had dropped the Winchester when he had been attacked from behind. He reloaded this, too, and then went hunting.

Danger wasn't far off. Three more Sioux warriors used ancient rifles to keep the mine's lone defender pinned down.

Slocum let out a war whoop of his own and started firing. In the darkness, his aim was poor. He might have hit one of the Indians. Thinking on it, Slocum decided he had missed by scant inches.

The attack sent the trio running into the night. Slocum almost collapsed in relief. He had attacked like a madman and had given the Sioux the idea they faced a dozen men instead of just one. If they found their four slain companions, they might just think a posse from Custer City had come to help the miners on the hill.

Slocum prowled around, but the Sioux had turned tail and run. He heaved a sigh of relief. He was dog tired and in no condition to keep fighting much longer. His ammunition was low, and the darkness favored the Indians.

He hunkered down behind a rock and shouted up to the miners, "My name's Slocum. I just ran the Sioux war party off. Can I come up?"

He didn't get an answer.

"This isn't a trick. I was on my way along the Cut-Off Trail, going to Custer City, when I saw some miners killed by the Sioux. I heard a woman scream and came to help out."

"How do I—we—know you're telling the truth?"

"You the one who screamed earlier?" he asked, thinking the woman's voice was similar in timbre. There might be an entire community or what was left of one up in the mine.

"How do we know you're not in league with those savages?"

"You don't. All I can give is my word. I don't rightly blame you, considering all you've been through. Just don't shoot. I'm going to fetch my horse and ride on to Custer City. I don't think the Sioux will bother you again."

"Wait!"

Slocum paused. Only the one woman spoke. He turned and stared up at the dark opening of the mine shaft.

"If you like, I can tell the sheriff in Custer City what's happened and have him send back a posse to help."

"I—I need help now," came the plaintive cry. "Th-they're dead. All of th-them."

"Just don't shoot. I'll come up and see what I can do."
Slocum stepped from the protecting rock and waited a few
seconds to show he wasn't trying to rush the mine's defend-
ers. Most of all, he didn't want someone getting spooked
and using him for target practice. It worked both ways. The
miners didn't have to trust him, but he didn't trust them,
either.

He started up the slope, his shoulder blades itching in
anticipation of a Sioux war lance from behind. And from
above? He might not be able to expect any better from the
miners. But he had to try to help. He had come this far.
There wasn't any reason to turn back now.

3

Slocum kept his hands away from his body. He worried that the woman up in the mine would get spooked when she saw the rifle in his left hand. He considered dropping it on his way to the mine but quickly forgot that. If the Sioux returned, he wanted as much firepower as he could muster. Halfway up the steep slope, he turned and looked back down at the base of the hill.

"What's wrong? What are you doing?" the woman above him demanded. Her voice was frightened. Slocum didn't like that. Frightened people made mistakes that might cost lives—in this case, his life.

"Just checking the area," Slocum said. "I don't want any of the Sioux war party to follow me up the hill."

"I don't see anything moving out there but you."

"That's good," Slocum said. "As long as you know there's no danger." He wanted her to be secure in the belief that he wasn't going to hurt her. By the time he got to the mouth of the mine, he was winded. It was a hell of a steep hill.

"You stay out there where I can see you clearly," came the tremulous command.

Slocum couldn't see the woman inside the mine, but he knew where she had to be. The crudely dug shaft pinched in within a few feet of the mouth. She was just behind a wood support for the roof. He took the chance to get his breath back.

"You all right, ma'am?" he asked. "Are there others here?"

"Why do you ask?" The question was both sharp and suspicious.

"If anyone's wounded, I might be able to fix 'em up. I've had my share of experience with gunshots."

The reaction he got was completely unexpected. The woman burst out crying. He saw a moment's glint off the blued rifle barrel as she fell forward to her knees. He advanced cautiously, not sure what to expect from the woman. She knelt and leaned forward, face buried in her hands. She wept openly.

"What's wrong?" he asked. He bit his tongue when he saw the men stacked like cordwood behind her in the mine. It was obvious what had happened. He counted no fewer than four bodies. The Sioux had done a good job on the miners.

"My entire family," she sobbed out. She looked up at him, tears rolling down her cheeks and leaving dirty streaks. The woman was in her early twenties and had hair blacker than coal. For a moment, Slocum thought she had herself under control. Then her blue eyes welled up with tears and spilled a new flood. She dabbed at the teardrops with the edge of a gingham apron. It only smeared the grime and made her look even more miserable.

Slocum said nothing as he went to examine the bodies. From the way they lay unmoving, he didn't think any were still alive. He had to check, though, just to be sure. Two of the bodies were stiff with rigor mortis. The other two were starting to decay. Their deaths had come many hours earlier.

"How long you been holed up in here?"

"Almost a day," she said, sniffing and rubbing her nose with the tip of her apron. She stood. Slocum was a little surprised. She was just a few inches under his six-foot height. She was a handsome, tall woman who had endured too much this day.

"The Sioux attacked just after dawn," he said, piecing it together. The miners he had found along the Cut-Off Trail had been dead a spell, possibly since dawn.

"That's right," she said. The crying had stopped, and she pulled her shoulders back. "My husband was the first to die. They caught him on his way up here to relieve my two brothers. I don't know what happened with my uncle. He—he came crawling in sometime after noon. He was more dead than alive then."

"Come on now," Slocum said. "There's nothing more we can do here." He tried to steer her away from the corpses. She jerked free and stood defiantly.

"We must bury them. *I* will bury them. There's no need for you to go to the trouble. You've already done more than could be expected from a stranger."

"The ground's mighty rocky," Slocum said dubiously. Digging four graves would take hours. It wasn't work he looked forward to.

"That's all right. This old mine's worthless. They hit galena and thought it might have a vein of gold. The mother lode, to hear Hans tell it."

"Your husband?"

She nodded. She straightened a little more and thrust out her hand. "I am Glorieta Zimmermann." Slocum shook her hand, not surprised at the strong grip.

"The mine's no good?" He looked around and saw where the miners had drilled core samples from the walls. The spongy rock looked like a piece of decayed and moldy bread, entirely wrong for the quartz bearing gold.

"They didn't know about mining. They thought they did." Glorieta took a deep breath and continued her futile chore of getting the grime off her cheeks. "It was all my husband's doing. We had a good business in Chicago. A yard goods store. It was not getting us anywhere, he said. We should go and get rich. My brothers and uncle believed him." She sniffed a final time and said, "Hans was always good at convincing people black was white."

Glorieta Zimmermann turned and walked away, not looking back. Slocum followed her from the mine and just watched. She went to a small cache drilled into the rock beside the mouth of the mine and lugged out a case of dynamite.

"Why didn't you use that against the Indians?" Slocum asked. A few sticks of dynamite with a foot of miner's black fuse would have scattered the Sioux.

"Hans did not want to waste it," she said almost primly. Slocum started to volunteer to help but then realized she knew what she was doing. He stood to one side and watched her expertly crimp the blasting caps and affix a yard of the waxy black fuse. She looked up, her blue eyes glowing in the dark. "Do you have a lucifer?"

Slocum silently lit one and handed the guttering match to her. She applied it to the fuse.

"We have two minutes to get away," she said. "I watched Hans most carefully. One foot equals one minute, and I cut a two-foot length."

Slocum took her arm and hurried her along. Glorieta walked as if she were in a trance. When the mouth of the mine erupted with dust and flying stone, her men were permanently buried.

Glorieta turned and stared at the rising cloud of debris. Then she broke down and cried again. Slocum put his arm around her quaking shoulders and held her close.

"We'd better be getting out of here. I didn't kill all the Sioux. I just chased them off. If they think on it, they'll realize they weren't up against the cavalry. I don't want to be here when they do."

"We can leave when I pack. I have no desire to stay in this godforsaken place. It was Hans's dream, not mine."

She sniffed loudly and blew her nose in the rumpled apron, then took it off and dropped it on the ground without even glancing down. It was a final gesture, a symbol of a life being abandoned. Glorieta stumbled and then let Slocum help her toward a rude stone hut stuck into the side of the steep hill. The walls were made from stone chiseled from the mine. Mortar and mud had been used to chink up the spaces between the unmatched rock. The floor was more rock than dirt, uneven and hard to stand on for very long.

For a roof someone had strung canvas between the walls. Looking up, Slocum saw stars through the tattered fabric. In a rain, it would be useless for protection.

"Haven't been here too long, have you?" he asked.

"We have only arrived this past fortnight," Glorieta said, taking out a carpetbag and stuffing her belongings into it. She picked up some items, then dropped them, only to pick them up again and just stare. Slocum knew the signs of shock when he saw them. Glorieta Zimmermann wasn't making good decisions right now, not after losing her entire family.

"You have relatives back in Chicago?" he asked. She just shook her head. "Nobody at all? Maybe somewhere else?"

"My ma died of smallpox. My papa fell under a harvester and was crushed nigh onto ten years back. I was just eleven then. The rest of the family's buried under a ton of that damned worthless rock!"

Her entire body shook. Slocum wondered what he had gotten himself into. Glorieta was in no condition to go rushing off into the night, especially when they might have to dodge the very Sioux Slocum had already run off. Those braves would have blood in their eyes and be looking for a white man's scalp—and his squaw.

"I reckon we can leave in the morning. There's no need to decide now what all to take."

Glorieta looked up at him, relief on her face. "Really? Thank you, sir."

"Call me John," Slocum said.

"And you may call me Glorieta. I am in your debt, sir— John."

Slocum stirred uncomfortably and looked around the cramped quarters. He wasn't sure what the sleeping arrangements had been. He saw only the one makeshift bed.

Glorieta saw his confusion. "They worked around the clock," she supplied. "My brothers put in twelve-hour shifts, then my uncle and Hans relieved them for the next twelve. There was no need for more than this bed." She stared at it as if she had never seen it before.

Glorieta moved as if in a dream and sat on the edge of the

bed. She looked up at Slocum, her eyes bigger and brighter and bluer than any he had ever seen before.

"Don't leave me alone tonight, John. Please. I—I couldn't bear it."

"Your husband's just died," he pointed out. "It's not right."

"It is," she insisted. "Hans was always going off on these crazy snipe hunts of his. I so seldom—saw him." She reached out and gripped Slocum's arm, pulling him firmly toward her. "I need you tonight. I *need* you."

There was no denying her. Slocum knew the danger of getting involved with a new widow, but he couldn't stop himself. It had been a powerful long time out on the trail and Glorieta Zimmermann was a handsome woman. Their lips met and crushed together with a mounting passion that sent Slocum's heart racing.

He reached out and cupped her breast. The woman's heart was beating even faster than his. His hand moved slowly in a circular motion. Glorieta's breathing became even more strained. She broke off and said, "I need you, John. Please, I need you now!"

He dropped his gun belt and kicked free of his boots. As he undressed, he watched Glorieta strip off her clothing. She was even more beautiful than he had thought. The worry and loss of the day seemed to vanish with her dress, and she lay naked on the simple bed, legs slightly parted, waiting for him.

Finished pulling off his long johns, Slocum sat on the edge of the bed, his fingertips lightly dancing over the curves of her body. The moon had risen and poked silver beams through the holes in the canvas roof. The light turned Glorieta's body to quicksilver.

He bent over and gently kissed first one and then the other nipple. The rubbery nubs were throbbing with life. He pressed his tongue down hard into one and felt the pounding of her heart. Sucking, he took in more of the luscious flesh. He teased the nipple trapped in his mouth with his tongue until the woman's back arched up off the bed and she moaned softly.

"Want me to stop?" he asked, pulling back when she gasped.

"No!"

The emphatic cry rang through the small stone hut and down the canyon. Slocum worried that the Sioux might have heard. Then he wasn't worrying about anything. Glorieta's long arms reached out and circled his neck and pulled him down to her.

Side by side they lay on the bed, their bodies rubbing slowly against each other. Their desires mounted, and it was Slocum's turn to cry out when the woman reached down and gripped his fleshy length. She squeezed hard. He wanted to explode.

"In a while," he said, moving her hand away. "It's been a spell for me. I want to do this right."

"You are, John. You are doing it right," she sighed. Glorieta turned slightly and lifted her leg over his hip. Both on their sides, face to face, they kissed and stroked and explored each other until there was no way either could hold back. Slocum moved closer and Glorieta hiked her leg even farther over his hip.

They gasped in unison when he moved slightly and found the moist, willing target. The dark-haired woman buried her face in his shoulder. He thought she was going to start crying. Instead she said, "Move, damn you. Don't stop now. I need you, I need to forget!"

He reached over her and gripped a firm buttock. He pulled her firmly in to his groin. Their crotches began grinding in small circles. He felt himself tightening, his balls turning to powder kegs ready to explode.

Glorieta's leg pulled him even closer as he began sliding in and out. He squeezed more firmly on the fleshy grip until she arched her back and shoved down hard. He buried himself as far into her steamy interior as he could. Surrounded by female warmth, squeezed down on all sides, Slocum let himself go. The age-old motion of a man and woman together took control of him and he lost himself in the blasting warmth from his loins.

The woman gasped and crushed herself to him even

harder. Then Glorieta relaxed and lay back, eyes open and staring up at the canvas roof.

"It'll get better, won't it, John?"

"I thought it was pretty durn good," he said, his hand resting on her warm belly.

"Not that," she said. "Life. It'll get better, won't it?"

Slocum didn't have any answer for her.

4

Slocum awoke with a start. His nose wrinkled at the smell of strong coffee brewing. He reached for his side arm, remembering too late that he had left the Colt in his holster—and the holster had been taken off before the night spent so pleasurably with Glorieta. He propped himself up on one elbow and took a look around the small stone hut.

The woman bent over a tiny cooking fire. She sensed him stirring and turned, a battered black coffeepot in her hand.

"Good morning, John. Coffee?"

"Reckon so," he said, thoughts of the Sioux still running through his mind. He heaved himself out of the bed, twisted to get the kinks out of his back, and quickly dressed. He made sure his cross-draw holster was settled comfortably on his hip. Today might be a repeat of all that had happened yesterday.

He silently took the tin coffee cup from Glorieta, their fingers touching slightly. She looked at him boldly. Her blue eyes taunted him, almost daring him to further action like the night before. This wasn't what Slocum needed now. He wanted to get into Custer City, get Glorieta settled or on her way back to Chicago, and then get on with his work. Finding the right place to hold up the gold-laden stagecoach running the three hundred miles between Deadwood and

Cheyenne would take some doing. He had to be wary of not only the law and the Sioux but also of the other outlaw bands. Being a robber wasn't easy in Dakota Territory.

"Good coffee," he said, draining the cup.

"Would you care for some breakfast? We don't have much. Hans—" Glorieta's voice trailed off. She had been trying to keep the memory of her dead husband from intruding. She had failed.

"Don't eat much in the morning," Slocum lied. He was hungry enough to eat a cow, moo and all. "We'd best get a move on. I don't want to spend any more time around here than I have to."

"I understand. While you slept, I finished packing." Glorieta indicated the carpetbag. Slocum couldn't tell if she had added any more to it than she had stuffed in the night before. It didn't matter. She was turning away from this desperate attempt to strike it rich. All gold mining had brought her was misery. He thought it was for the best if she tried to forget rather than hang onto keepsakes that would force her to remember.

"Let's get on the trail," he said, standing. Slocum hefted her bag and took it outside. It was then that he remembered he had left his sorrel down the canyon a ways. He hoped the Sioux had missed her. The horse was dependable and the closest thing to a friend he'd had in the past three months.

To his immense relief the Sioux war party had not found the animal. The sorrel tossed her head and stared at him askance, as if demanding to know where he had been for so long. Slocum loosened the reins and let the horse graze farther from the spot where she had already cropped the sere grass.

"I'm ready, John," Glorieta said, head high and shoulders back.

Except for the redness in her eyes, Slocum would never have been able to tell that this woman had lost anyone near and dear to her. She put up a brave front for his benefit. Or was it for her own benefit? Slocum wasn't sure whether or not Glorieta maintained the rigid iron expression to keep from uncontrollably bawling her eyes out.

He swung up into the saddle, then pulled Glorieta up behind him. He enjoyed the feel of her arms around his waist as they slowly made their way back to the Cut-Off Trail, but as they neared Custer City, Slocum became more and more edgy. He didn't know what he was going to do with her. Glorieta had no money, and he had damned little himself. That was one reason he wanted to separate a few ounces of gold from its rightful owner.

"Why do you come this way, John?"

He started to tell her, then held back. They had spent the night together. That didn't make them anything more than two people who had shared a night of misery to keep from thinking about worse things. He cleared his throat and told her the half of his reason for coming to Custer City that didn't fully reveal his larcenous intent.

"The challenge. I always enjoy a challenge. It's here." He looked around the main street in Custer City and shook his head. Every third building was a saloon. The few stores sandwiched between tended to supply the miners. More than one general store was in sight along the main street, along with a bakery, a seamstress, an undertaker, and the assay office. Of the stores, Slocum guessed the undertaker got the most business. It was hard and dangerous work being a miner.

"Do you know anyone here?" she asked.

"Might. My friends move around a good deal." He didn't add that they were usually one step ahead of the law when they decided to move on.

"We hadn't been here long enough. Hans and I passed through here so fast I hardly had time to look in the windows."

"You any good at sewing?" Slocum asked. The seamstress shop might be a good place for Glorieta if she could use a needle.

"No, not really."

"You said you ran a store back in Chicago. You might ask around and see if any of the shopkeepers need help."

There was a long pause. He felt her arms stiffen around

his waist. Then she said in a low, choked voice, "I thought I could stay with you."

"Let's get bedded down for the night," Slocum said. The five hours it had taken the tired horse to get them to town had worn out the sorrel. Slocum was feeling a bit peaked himself, and he still had a spell of looking around to do before he was ready to turn in. All the way into Custer City he had thought of the armored stagecoach and the barrage fired from it into the band of road agents. Somebody had declared war on highwaymen and he had to find out who it was before he got down to serious robbing.

The best way of doing that was to drift from one saloon to another and keep his ears open. The miners would try to drown the sorrow of their lost mother lodes, ease the aching of their tired muscles, and generally get stinking drunk before returning to their work the next morning. A clever man could learn a great deal simply by buying a drink or two and listening hard.

"There is a hotel," Glorieta said, pointing down the street. "It does not appear to be too expensive."

"Everything in Custer City is going to be higher than a cat's back," Slocum said. He had been in boomtowns before and knew how the proprietors overcharged mercilessly. They had to make their killing before the veins of ore turned to worthless rock.

"I have a few dollars—"

"That's all right. Let's get settled and see." Slocum negotiated with the hotel clerk for ten minutes before agreeing on a price of five dollars in gold for the night. Even in Denver at the Palmer House he could have gotten a better room for a cheaper price. And this tumbledown shack was hardly the opulent palace with liveried servants that the Palmer House was.

Slocum lugged his gear and Glorieta's carpetbag up the rickety stairs and found the room at the top of the flight. He dropped everything on the bed and said, "You get things squared away. I've got some business to attend to."

"But you said you didn't know anyone in Custer City."

Slocum's cold green eyes stopped Glorieta from questioning him further. He didn't want her hanging around his neck like a millstone. He felt responsible for her, and he knew he shouldn't. The fight with the Sioux had been short and savage. If he hadn't come along when he had, Glorieta would have been kidnapped by the war party. He knew what they did with white women—and he suspected Glorieta knew, too. She was a handsome woman and was far from being stupid.

"Don't worry. I'll be back." He pointed to his bedroll. "You've got everything I own there. I'll be back."

She threw her arms around his neck and caught him by surprise with the quick kiss.

"I'll be here, John. I'll be waiting for you."

He nodded absently and left, more worried than ever about her. There was no way in hell he could have her sticking this close to him if he got down to serious business. A few small robberies or one good one and he'd be off for the Canadian border, maybe with a posse hot on his heels. He didn't want her along. It wasn't fair to her after all she had lost.

Slocum wandered down the street, now thronged with miners. Damned near six thousand men crowded Custer City. Slocum stepped back into shadow when a group of men came pounding hard down the street. From the way they rode together, he pegged them as vigilantes.

"That there's Captain Jack," came a soft voice. "Him and the Custer Minutemen keep the redskins from stealin' too many horses. The Sioux been raidin' in the area."

Slocum turned and saw an old man, sitting in a chair propped back against a wall. He hadn't noticed the man before he'd spoken.

"Who's Captain Jack?"

"Jack Crawford. A fine man," the old geezer said, spitting into the street. "He's a government scout. Got a hundred twenty-five men or more what ride with him. They keep trouble to a minimum here." The old man settled down a bit more comfortably in the chair and asked, "You lookin' for trouble?"

"What makes you think that?"

The man laughed. "That six-shooter of yours has a used look about it. Most of the men rushin' into Custer City wouldn't know what end of a hogleg to hold. You ain't got that problem."

"Maybe not, but I do have a problem."

"What's that?" the man asked, craning his neck a mite to get a better look at Slocum.

"I worked up a powerful thirst along the Cut-Off Trail. Which of all these saloons is the best?"

"Don't much matter, but you might give the Blue Ox a try. There's men there you might find—friendly."

Slocum thanked the man and started off in the direction of the nearby saloon. He stepped into the smoky main room of the saloon and saw immediately what the old man had meant. Although there were miners here, most of the clientele looked more like the vultures that lived off the miners' carcasses. Slocum might want to palaver with a few outlaws later on, when he had a better notion of what was happening in Dakota Territory, but right now, he wanted to talk with the men who pulled the gold from the ground.

He backed out of the Blue Ox and started down the wide main street. For a town of six thousand, there must have been a saloon for every thirty residents. Slocum found a saloon more to his liking. The Yosemite was crowded with miners, all intent on dropping their leather pouches filled with gold dust onto the bar for the barkeep to weigh out a portion and hand back a bottle filled with dubious liquor.

Slocum saw with a single glance how the barkeep was shortchanging the miners. The man's long fingernails scooped up enough gold dust to rob them of a dollar every time they dropped dust into his balance pans. Stuck in a cutting block was a knife the barkeep used now and again to clean his nails. The grimy, gold-dust-laden parings were pushed back under the bar for later recovery.

"What'll this buy me?" Slocum asked, dropping a greenback on the bar.

The barkeep sneered. "Not too damn much. We can swap that for a trade dollar."

"A five-dollar greenback for a single trade dollar?"

Slocum wasn't unduly surprised, though he feigned it.

"A trade dollar gets you a bottle of the best we got in the Yosemite."

"Do it," Slocum said. He wasn't going to drink much of the rotgut. He wanted it to loosen other tongues.

"You look as if you'd be more at home down at the Blue Ox," the barkeep said. He popped the cork from the bottle of trade whiskey he gave Slocum.

"There's enough thievin' going on here to keep me happy," Slocum said, staring significantly at the barkeep's nails. The thought darted across his mind that enough gold dust might be spilled on the floor to make the muck under the Yosemite Saloon a veritable gold mine of its own. Slocum pushed this from his mind. That was too much like work—and he didn't doubt that the barkeep and the saloon's owner jealously guarded any additional source of revenue.

Slocum sipped at the whiskey, trying not to make a face. It had rusted nails and gunpowder added to it to give color and body. From the bite, he thought the barkeep might have also added some nitric acid. There wasn't anyone else in the huge room that was likely to complain about the quality, though. The whiskey had enough alcohol in it to stun a mule.

Slocum bided his time and found a grizzled old miner well on his way to getting soused. He went over to the man's table and asked if he could sit down.

"Do I know you?" the miner asked suspiciously, closing one eye and squinting to focus better.

"I'm the man who's going to buy you another drink," Slocum said. He had brought a second shot glass with him from the bar. The invitation was instantly seized.

"My long lost brother!" the miner crowed. "It's been years."

"How's the mine coming along? Good enough to drink to?" Slocum waited for the response. The long face and slight shaking of the head indicated this man's mine wasn't producing much in the way of wealth. Slocum didn't care

about that. He wanted gossip. Who was doing the best?
How did they get their treasure to the Deadwood smelters?

"I'm drinkin' to forget, not to celebrate," the man said.
"That good-for-nothing Jeremiah Carson done bought me
out for a song."

"You must be sitting pretty then," Slocum said.

"I ain't. My mine didn't pan out because I can't dig deep
enough by myself. Carson's got a dozen men working for
him. They got drills and some fancy-ass mining engineer
from France working with them. He's buyin' every damn
claim he can find. Gonna be rich, he is—and off *my*
claim!"

Slocum kept the liquor flowing and the words pouring
after. He formed a picture of the community and of Jeremiah
Carson. If anyone was shipping gold to Deadwood, it would
be the land-grabbing Mr. Carson. When the bottle was
empty, he pushed back from the table. He had enough
information to get started.

As he stood and turned toward the swinging doors,
Slocum froze. The man standing in the doorway had a hand
on his six-shooter. And Slocum knew him for the killer that
he was. Their eyes locked and Slocum heard the din in the
saloon drop to a deathly silence as everyone waited for one
or the other of the gunmen to draw.

5

Slocum moved so that his feet were wider than usual. The stance gave him all the stability he needed for the quick draw and a rapid, accurate first shot. His left hand pulled back his canvas duster and left his Colt Navy free on his hip. The hatchet-faced man with the long black mustaches in the doorway moved his feet in the same way. His large, steady hand hovered over the worn butt of a six-shooter.

"Slocum, you son of a bitch," the man said in a voice colder than any polar storm.

"It's been a while, Goodale." Slocum's reply was no less chilling. Men all around him in the saloon began backing away, waiting for the lead to start flying.

"Damn right it has been."

"Hey, gents, go on out into the street, will you?" called the barkeep. Slocum saw from the corner of his eye that the man had both hands under the bar. Slocum didn't doubt there was a sawed-off shotgun resting there. If it looked as if lead would start flying, the barkeep would be able to cut down both gunmen and save a few of the Yosemite's customers.

"He's tellin' us to leave, ain't he, Slocum?" Goodale turned and faced the barkeep.

"I heard it that way, too," Slocum said. "He must not want our business."

"Then let's get on down to the Blue Ox. You owe me a drink, and I mean to collect it."

Slocum walked forward slowly. The crowd in the Yosemite Saloon didn't know what to expect. A huge collective breath was released when Slocum slapped Doug Goodale on the back and the gunman did likewise. Goodale held the door open for Slocum.

"It's been a spell, hasn't it, Slocum?"

"Well nigh two years," Slocum said. He and Doug Goodale had ridden together for almost a month down Santa Fe way. Goodale had been daring to the point of recklessness. Slocum didn't cotton to having his head blown off because some damned fool liked to spray lead around— and this seemed to happen a great deal when Goodale led a robbery. Other than the brashness, Goodale was a decent enough person and Slocum liked him. He just didn't want to throw in with him unless the robbery sounded too good to pass up.

"What are you doin' in these here parts, John?"

"I reckon about the same as you are," Slocum said. They walked along the crowded street, avoiding the drunks staggering from one saloon to another.

"Why's that?" Doug Goodale asked after they reached the doors leading into the Blue Ox Saloon.

"Gold."

Goodale laughed heartily. "I might have known you'd sniff out the Deadwood Treasure Coach. That's a scent so powerful it's drawin' men from all over the West."

Slocum didn't rightly know what Goodale meant, but he was willing to let him keep talking. He certainly liked the sound of "treasure coach." It might even have something to do with the ambush he had seen the lawmen make on the band of road agents.

"Here's a chair," Goodale said, shoving a drunk miner to the floor. The man curled up into a tight ball and snored loudly, never noticing his fall from grace.

Goodale and Slocum sat. A bottle magically appeared,

and to Slocum's delight, it wasn't trade whiskey. This was smooth and puddled warmly in his guts. He licked the rim of the glass and indicated he wouldn't mind sampling a bit more from Goodale's bottle.

"Powerful stuff, John. Don't let it sneak up on you."

"I've been drinking gunpowder and nitric acid over at the other saloon. This is liquor I can really drink."

Doug Goodale laughed. "This is the kind of booze we'll both be swilling if the robbery comes off right."

"Don't go telling me anything you shouldn't," said Slocum, aware that Goodale enjoyed bragging. If he had any partners in this proposed robbery, they might not take kindly to him shooting his mouth off in front of an outsider.

"I'm still gettin' the men together for it, John. This is going to be the robbery of the century."

"The Deadwood Treasure Coach," Slocum said, enjoying the feel of it on his tongue. "What is it?"

"You don't know?" Goodale's eyebrows arched up. He stared at Slocum for a moment, then laughed. "That's rich. I thought you were lookin' to get to it before I did."

"I saw a stagecoach loaded with a dozen armed men out on the road. Some highwaymen tried to waylay it and all hell broke loose."

Goodale snorted in contempt. "That stagecoach was out-fitted by Jack Crawford and his boys. They prowl the road waiting for men too dumb to know the difference between a trap and the mother lode. I tell you, Slocum, this is the real thing. The treasure coach needs six strong horses just to pull it. There's that much gold on it!"

"Anything posing that good a target will be well guard-ed."

"Not necessarily. They've got too much gold to protect. The stagecoach line, the Gilmer, Saulsbury, and Patrick Stage Company, do their damnedest but it's not good enough. Not by half. There's been eleven robberies so far in the past month, all of them successful." He grinned like the cat who had finished off the canary. Slocum guessed Goodale was doing a bit of bragging now.

"So you're saying we just ride up and relieve the stage-coach of its strongbox?" This sounded too incredible for Slocum to swallow. Goodale was overlooking something—or trying to make a bad situation sound better to get Slocum to agree to join in.

"Maybe not just like that. There's a sheriff who's makin' trouble for me already."

"Custer City? Or from Deadwood?"

"Not from this nothing hole in the wall," said Doug Goodale, sneering in contempt. "Look, Slocum, it's a sweet deal, but it needs good men to pull it off. I got the place picked out. I been scoutin' for more than two weeks. The gold leaves the smelter in Deadwood and ends up in Cheyenne. There's no reason why just one load shouldn't end up in *our* pockets."

Slocum sipped at his liquor and thought on it. He had come to Dakota Territory for such an opportunity. He respected Doug Goodale's planning ability. The man had a keen eye for good robbery possibilities. Slocum would have liked the situation much better if he hadn't ridden with Goodale before and known how reckless he was in the actual execution of the robbery. Goodale's contempt for the law prompted him to do senseless killing. Slocum preferred getting in and out with as little bloodshed as possible. A man might be mad if you robbed him of his gold, but a relative would get pissed off and track you to the ends of the earth if you killed a brother or uncle or father.

"Who else is in on this?" asked Slocum. He would have to make his decision on the caliber of the men Goodale had recruited.

"So you're interested, eh?" The man's hatchet face widened in a smile. "I thought you were my man, Slocum. You always did know a good thing when you saw it."

"I'm not joining you—not yet. I need to know more. Some of us aren't quite as impetuous as others."

"There's not much more I can tell you without giving away some inside information," Goodale said. "You're going to have to trust me—or we're going to be competitors for the coach."

"Wouldn't want that," Slocum said, making up his mind. Doug Goodale was a good man as long as the heat of a robbery didn't get him too fired up. Slocum thought that could be dealt with later.

"So?"

"So count me in. This is why I came to this part of the country."

Goodale slapped Slocum on the shoulder and said, "Let's drink to seal the deal. We're gonna get rich, John. I promise it."

They had just knocked back shots of liquor when the doors of the saloon crashed back and a tall woman burst through. Several of the men at the bar were reaching for their side arms. They relaxed when they saw Glorieta Zimmermann. She wasn't armed and posed no threat to them.

"Hey, babe, come on over here. I'll show you a good time, a damn good time!" called one. The others picked up the cry and shouted lewd suggestions to her.

Glorieta ignored them and homed in on Slocum.

"Why are you here?" he asked before she could speak.

"She with you, John? You did have a way with women," Goodale said. Slocum knew he fancied himself a ladies' man. Glorieta had cleaned herself up and presented a pretty picture among the few scrawny whores working in the Blue Ox.

"John, you've got to leave immediately."

"There's no need—" Goodale stopped speaking when he saw the storm cloud crossing Slocum's face.

"You shouldn't be in here," Slocum told Glorieta. "Why'd you leave the hotel?"

"I—I was bored, John. And it's a good thing I walked around a bit, too. I overheard him. He's coming here for you."

"Who's coming here?" Slocum's heart pounded. He had too many warrants out to count. Anyone might have come across one and seen the price on his head. "For me?"

"Well, not for you. Leastwise, he didn't mention you by name, John. The sheriff's coming *here* to clean the place out. Everyone in Custer City knows the Blue Ox Saloon is a hangout for crooks." Glorieta looked around the large room, as if just aware of the kind of men coming to this saloon to drink.

"Start over," Slocum said, calming down. "Who's coming here?"

"The Deadwood sheriff."

"Seth Bullock!" cried Goodale. "He's been hot on my trail for two weeks."

"He doesn't want me?" Slocum asked Glorieta. "He didn't mention me by name?"

"No, but he described your friend. Are you Doug Goodale?" she asked.

"Shit, Bullock *is* onto me. Son of a bitch." Goodale jumped up so fast his chair tipped over. "Meet me in Deadwood in a week, Slocum. We'll—" Goodale never got any farther. A bullet sang through the air and ripped off his hat.

Slocum drew and fired. His slug joined a dozen others from those inside the saloon. He knew he wasn't the only one running from the law. The old man back on the porch had intimated that the Blue Ox was a place where outlaws hung out. He had been right.

"Give it up, Goodale!" came the loud cry from outside. "I've got a posse with me. You'll never get out of there alive. We'll burn the damn place to the ground if we have to!"

Goodale was already racing up the stairs to the second floor. Slocum saw the heavily barred door at the back of the saloon. The posse wasn't going to get through it easily. Men flocked to the front of the saloon, pistols blazing wildly. They didn't have good targets, but it didn't matter to them. It would be only seconds before Bullock and his men returned fire with a vengeance.

"John, what—"

Slocum didn't stay to answer Glorieta. He grabbed her hand and jerked her behind him, protesting as they went. He followed Goodale up the stairs. Whatever escape route the outlaw had would be the best bet for Slocum and Glorieta, too.

At the head of the stairs Slocum slowed and looked around. The cribs were small, hardly wider than his shoulders. Each had a thin pallet on the floor. One on his left had a naked woman and a half-dressed miner just finishing their business. The room didn't have a window. He looked into the room on the right. It didn't have a window, either.

"There, John. Your friend's gone through there!" Glorieta pointed.

Slocum dragged her along toward the narrow, high window set in the hallway. The glass had been smashed. He heard the heavy pounding of footsteps on the saloon roof. He knew Goodale had no more than a few seconds' head start on them. He just hoped Goodale tried to escape rather than take a parting shot at Sheriff Bullock. If he did that, he would draw the posse's fire, and Slocum would find himself the recipient of a leaden barrage.

"Up," he said to Glorieta. "Get through the window. Now!"

The gunfire in the saloon below had died down quickly. Bullock might have made it known that he was searching for only Doug Goodale. If so, the others might have decided to step back and let the lawman have his worthless prey.

Slocum heaved and boosted the tall woman up to the window. She kicked and wiggled and finally squeezed through the small window. From outside, Glorieta said something to Slocum that he didn't hear. The sound of boots pounding hard on the stairs demanded his immediate attention. The first man to the top was a deputy. The silver glint of light off his badge told Slocum all he needed about who came after him. He aimed and fired. The man yelped and dived back down the stairs. From the loud shouts and curses, Slocum knew the deputy had crashed into others in the posse who had followed him upstairs.

Jumping, Slocum pulled himself through the window.

They didn't have as good a chance of getting away as Goodale had. The posse knew their escape route. It would take only seconds before Bullock out in the street knew, too.

The roof sloped downward sharply. The small gable they had emerged from gave no protection from anyone in the street below. Slocum saw a half dozen men milling around. They had to be in Bullock's posse. Any second now they would look up and when they did, they'd open up with the rifles they carried.

"What are we going to do, John?"

"You shouldn't have come after me like that," he said. "We might not get out of this in one piece."

"You're an outlaw, aren't you?"

"Goodale is. Just being seen with him is enough to get my neck stretched by a lynch mob."

Slocum saw the only chance for escape, and it was a dangerous route. The slippery wood shingled roof sloped steeply and made solid footing a joke. But he had to try. To go down to the street teeming with lawmen was impossible.

"I'm going to try to jump to the next building," he told Glorieta. "You stay here and maybe they'll come after me and not see you."

"No!"

She pushed past him and jumped first. She sailed through the air. Her skirts fluttered wildly and made her appear to be some weird nocturnal bird. She flapped her arms for stability and crashed hard into the roof of the adjoining building.

Slocum hesitated after he saw that she had reached safety. If he had another way out, he would have let her go. She was better off without him and he knew he was better off without her. Glorieta Zimmermann didn't deserve being chased down by a posse.

The clatter of boots inside the narrow hall and the sound of six-shooters cocking convinced him there was no way he could escape other than to follow her.

He got to the edge of the roof, positioned himself, and

jumped. Just as he did, a shot rang out, and he felt the heel of his boot explode. He was in midair between the buildings, but he hadn't been able to push off hard enough. He was going to fall into the street, smack dab in the center of Bullock's posse.

6

Slocum flailed wildly as he fell between the two buildings. His feet kicked and his arms windmilled and he knew he wasn't going to reach the far building where Glorieta stood. He got a glimpse of her distraught expression—and of the dozen men in the street below. He didn't need to be told that the tall, heavyset man fifteen feet below was the Deadwood sheriff, Seth Bullock. Just the way the man carried himself so arrogantly told of power.

Everything moved slower than molasses for Slocum. His muscles wouldn't respond fast enough. His mind worked like lightning but his body dragged. He reached out, knowing he wasn't going to get to the haven offered by the other building.

"John!" Glorieta called. "Don't do it!"

He didn't know what she was telling him. He couldn't do anything but walk on thin air. Imperceptibly, the building came closer and closer. He leaned forward, arms straining hard. His fingers brushed the edge of the roof, a scant inch short.

He slipped down the side of the building, its rough planking ripping at his clothing.

The world snapped back into full-speed motion when Slocum slammed hard against the wall and just hung. For several seconds he didn't know what had happened. His fingers were cut and bloodied from trying to grab onto the edge of the roof. But now they weren't clinging to anything. He kicked his feet weakly.

"Your gun belt, John. It's caught!" cried Glorieta.

How he wished the woman would keep her mouth shut. She was drawing the attention of the posse in the street. He didn't need those vultures flocking around his carcass. Had Doug Goodale jumped the gap between the buildings and already fled? Slocum's mind refused to concentrate on the most important thing in the world: saving himself.

"Wait, John, I'll pull you up. Don't move!"

He knew he had only seconds before someone below started shooting. He pushed back as far from the wall as he could and saw the heavy nail that had snared his gun belt. His weight was pulling the nail free from the wall. Slocum looked around for something to grab. He was caught on the face of a bare wall. There weren't even windows to give his toes purchase.

"Here, take it. I can pull you up," called Glorieta. From somewhere she had fetched a short length of rope. The ends were tarred and sticky, but Slocum found this to be a benefit. The rope stuck to his palms and gave him a better grip. Just as Glorieta began pulling, the nail screeched free of the wall.

The abortive flight and the crashing against the wall hadn't alerted the posse. The nail pulling out of the wall did.

"There! Up there! That one's getting away!"

Bullets sent splinters flying around him. And all Slocum could do was let Glorieta pull him up. Inch by inch he went up the wall until he could grab the verge with both hands and heave himself over. He felt hot lead nick at his boot sole and knew he had barely made it.

And they still weren't clear. Sheriff Bullock and his deputies had spotted him.

"Thanks," Slocum said, peeling the tarry rope from his hands. "Another second and I'd've been flat on my back in the street."

"You'd've been dead," Glorieta corrected. She was flushed from exertion and the rosy spots on her cheeks heightened her beauty. He was glad she was a strong woman. A smaller one could never have pulled his dead weight up the side of the building as she had done.

"Still might be," Slocum said. "They saw me." Punctuating his words were more slugs winging loudly past the edge of the roof. He and Glorieta were out of sight, but that didn't stop the kill-crazy posse from firing at shadows.

"There," she said. "Over there is the way your friend got away. We can use it, too."

A small trapdoor opened into the attic of the building. Slocum knew they had only seconds before all hope for escape was gone. He dived headfirst through the opening and crashed into the attic. Glorieta helped him up and pointed silently. A waist-high section of paneling had been pulled free and not returned to its proper place.

"There's where your friend went," Glorieta said.

Slocum wasted no time pushing the woman into the small cubbyhole and following her. He tugged at the balky panel and pulled it shut behind him just as the thundering of feet on the narrow stairs told of the posse's arrival. Through cracks in the wall he was able to peer out and see the armed men struggling to get to the roof. The posse carried enough firepower to ventilate an army.

"There's a narrow staircase leading down, John."

"Go on," he urged. He followed Glorieta down and they came to the alley on the far side of the building. He didn't know why the stairs had been built and why they had been hidden, but he wasn't complaining. They had saved his life. He just wished that Doug Goodale had confided more in him. That he hadn't was typical. Goodale had a sneaky streak a mile wide.

Slocum shook his head as he took Glorieta's arm and hustled her along the street. He might be thinking uncharitable thoughts of Goodale that weren't deserved. There hadn't been time for Goodale to tell him much of anything. The way Bullock came after the outlaw told Slocum that Goodale was on to something big.

The Deadwood Treasure Coach. It had the ring of gold to it. Slocum liked that.

"We can't stay in town, John," said Glorieta. "The sheriff will be hunting for us."

"For me, not you," he said. Slocum thought on it. The sheriff never got a good look at him. The deputies had chased him because he had been drinking with Goodale. He knew he had to leave Custer City right away, though. He was a cautious sort when it came to getting arrested. The sheriff might turn the entire town upside down, but would he know who he was hunting for?

Slocum didn't want to jeopardize his chance of joining Goodale in the treasure coach heist.

"You stay in the hotel. I'd better hightail it into the hills where the sheriff isn't as likely to hunt for me."

Glorieta said nothing as they returned to the hotel and went up the stairs. The clerk slept behind the counter, snoring noisily. He wouldn't be able to give the sheriff any good information about his customers. If anything, he might lie to hide the fact that he'd been sleeping on the job. Slocum counted that as a lucky break.

"John, wait," Glorieta said when he started to put his few belongings into his bedroll.

"Don't argue. I've got to leave."

"Does the sheriff know you? Is there a wanted poster out on you?"

Slocum shrugged. This wasn't a good enough answer for Glorieta. She asked him again, "Can the sheriff identify you?"

"Reckon not. Leastwise, he didn't get too good a look before his deputies started firing. We took out after Goodale before too many lawmen got into the saloon."

"Then the posse is as likely to be able to identify me as you. They saw a woman with this Goodale friend of yours."

"Didn't say he was a friend. Not exactly."

"Your cohort, then," she said almost primly. "He is an outlaw, isn't he? And the pair of you are going to commit some crime."

"We talked about it," Slocum said carefully. "Does that bother you?"

From the light in her eyes he saw that it didn't bother her as much as it excited her. He let out a small sigh. He had found other women like this. They led easy lives, sheltered lives, dull lives filled with endless monotony of day-to-day chores. The thought of committing a crime, or just being with a road agent, thrilled them. It brought new definition to their lives. It *excited* them.

All Slocum wanted was to cut Glorieta loose. She was a lovely woman and had a spark of fire he appreciated, but she knew nothing about the life he lived. If she had been content to be the wife of a store owner and a miner, she would never be able to adapt to worrying about staying one step ahead of the law.

"They lynch gold thieves in these parts," Slocum said.

"What?" The sudden change in his argument took her aback.

"They hang thieves here." He related to her what he had seen on the road with the fake stagecoach that had lured the band of highwaymen close, then had turned into a deadly trap. "That was just a bunch of amateurs. Captain Jack Crawford and a bunch calling themselves the Custer Minutemen. From all I hear, Seth Bullock is one tough hombre. He isn't going to stop hunting Doug Goodale until he catches him, Goodale gets out of Dakota Territory, or he's dead."

"You won't get caught. You're good, John."

"How do you know?"

"I know. A woman knows about men. You're too smart."

"There are hundreds of cottonwoods around here with men dangling from them who thought they were smarter than the law."

"You are," Glorieta said, breathless. Slocum saw that she was caught up in what she thought was a glamorous life. No amount of telling her the truth about the danger and deprivation would sway her now. Slocum would have to ride on out and just abandon her. He hated doing it, but it was the most decent thing he could do.

He went to the small window and peered out. His hand darted toward his holstered Colt Navy. The street was filled with patrolling men. They all carried ax handles or shotguns. When Slocum saw the blue bandannas tied around their upper right forearms he knew they must be the Custer Minutemen using this simple uniform to mark their own ranks.

A man mounted on a huge black stallion trotted down the street, directing the vigilantes. As he turned, his horse reared. He held the powerful animal in check easily. Slocum saw the flash off the man's badge. This was Seth Bullock, the sheriff of Deadwood. He had said unkind things earlier about local sheriffs. He didn't want to repeat them in front of this man. He looked as if he was pretty damned good with the ivory-handled six-shooter hanging at his side.

"We can't get past them, John. They're everywhere."

Slocum saw two of the Custer Minutemen enter the hotel, shotguns resting in the crooks of their arms. He drew his Colt and reloaded the spent chambers. He waited for what seemed an eternity, ready to fight to the death if needed. When he saw the two vigilantes leave the hotel in disgust, he knew the clerk had lied about being awake all night and had chased them off.

He let out a sigh of relief, but he wasn't going anywhere tonight. Not with the whole damned town swarming with the sheriff's deputies and Crawford's vigilantes.

As if reading his thoughts, Glorieta said, "We don't have to waste the time, John. We can enjoy this fine bed. It's so much softer than the one we had up at the mine."

Her hands reached around his waist, stroking and touching him in ways he didn't want. He started to push her back, then relented when her hands moved lower and cupped the bulge at his crotch. She squeezed gently and began kneading. He stiffened to the point where staying in his trousers became almost painful.

"We can pass the time so much better here than out on the trail," she said. He turned and stared into her startlingly blue eyes. Slocum reached out and brushed a strand of her black hair back, then he kissed her. Their tongues danced back and forth, stroking and teasing and building passion.

Slocum felt her nimble fingers working harder at his crotch. He wanted to explode. She sensed his discomfort and the reason for it and unfastened his gun belt. He grabbed the ebony-handled Colt before the belt hit the floor. He placed the pistol on the small table beside the bed where he could get to it if he needed it in a hurry. He wanted Glorieta, but he hadn't forgotten the posse scouring the town. It never paid to let passion overwhelm prudence.

"Undress me, John. Do it real slow." Glorieta stepped back and let her arms hang limp at her sides. She closed her eyes and licked her lips. A toss of her head flung back the raven hair that had fallen across her eyes.

He stood and stared at her for a moment, drinking in her beauty. Then he began undressing her. The snaps and buttons came apart slowly. Silken white shoulders appeared as he pushed back the top of her dress. Glorieta shrugged once and the dress fell around her waist. He kept working at her undergarments. This time, though, he used his mouth as well as his fingers. His tongue untied only a few of the white satin ribbons holding her lacy camisole together. But it didn't matter. The light touch of his wet tongue against her bare flesh caused them both to shiver deliciously.

Getting the dress off around her hips afforded Slocum the chance to see her completely naked. Dim light from the street filtered through the window and turned her into a goddess hewn from ivory. His heart started beating faster and he felt the warmth mounting in his loins. He had to have her. Now.

He reached out and drew her warmth to him. Glorieta let out a tiny sigh and wiggled down beside him. The clothes she still had on vanished like mist in the warm spring sun. Her fingers stroked and teased and got him out of his useless clothing.

"Yes, John," she whispered hotly in his ear. "I want you. I want you so much!"

He kissed her hard, his tongue probing into her mouth.

She strained to crush her body as tightly against his as possible. He felt her lush breasts flatten. The hard points of her nipples poked into him and spurred him on.

Together they rolled over onto the bed, Slocum ending up on top. The woman's long legs opened for him. He moved, the tip of his manhood touching the moist warmth of the furry nest between her legs. Glorieta shivered in anticipation.

Slocum held back for a moment to savor the sensations coursing through him.

"Don't, John," she pleaded. "Don't you dare stop. I need you. I need you *inside* me!"

He wasn't going to stop. He just wanted to relish the way he felt at the moment. His hips moved slightly. The end of his fleshy shaft entered her. A shudder passed through Glorieta like a warm, silky wind blowing through the tall pines. She arched her back and tried to ram herself fully onto his hardness. Only when Slocum was ready did he give her what she wanted.

He quickly found it was also exactly what he wanted—needed.

He gasped as he sank balls deep into her. Glorieta's legs rose on either side and circled his waist. She locked her heels behind him and trapped him completely. He was past caring. His hips levered back and forth in the age-old rhythm of a man loving a woman. Together their passions mounted until both exploded.

Glorieta let out a tiny trapped animal sigh, then relaxed. Her eyelids grew heavy and drooped. In minutes she was asleep. Slocum disengaged from her embrace and padded softly to the window. Cold air sneaked around the poorly fitting window and chilled him. He hardly noticed. His gaze was too firmly fixed on the posse still patrolling the street below.

He turned and looked back at the sleeping woman. If the posse had been gone, would he have left her?

He returned to bed. His arms enveloped her and within a few minutes he, too, was sound asleep.

7

Slocum stared out the hotel room window and wondered if any of the people going about their business down in the street were members of Sheriff Bullock's posse. He couldn't tell the lawmen from the ordinary citizens now that the sun had crept up over the hills and Custer City had begun stirring.

He cinched the gunbelt tight around his waist and stared at the peacefully sleeping Glorieta Zimmermann. He didn't know what the hell to do with her. She had saved him and didn't seem upset at the notion he and Doug Goodale were in cahoots. Still, rescuing him from a berserk lawman at the head of a lynch mob and helping him rob a bank— or the Deadwood Treasure Coach—was another matter. Glorieta struck him as the law-abiding sort. If anyone had approached her a few weeks earlier with the notion of helping in a gold shipment robbery, she would have turned him in to the law.

Picking up his gear, he walked on cat's feet to the door, intending to leave her. He had to get out of town before Bullock found him or Captain Crawford and his vigilantes started nosing around. Slocum lived with the knowledge of all the wanted posters bearing his likeness. The rewards for his various crimes might not be great, but even fifty dollars could get a man killed in Dakota Territory.

"John, are you leaving me?"

Slocum stopped. He had been as quiet as he could, but she had still heard him.

"It's for the best, Glorieta. You don't belong with me."

"I'm not good enough?"

"It's not that." Slocum swung around and dropped his bedroll and saddlebags to the floor. He couldn't just walk out on her. Staring into her big blue eyes robbed him of what little resolve he had on the matter.

"Then what is it?" She sat up in bed, letting the sheet fall down just enough to expose her naked breasts. Slocum realized she was using every trick possible to make him stay. He also realized the tricks were working.

"I saved you back at the mine. You saved me here in town. That makes us even. I don't owe you anything, and you don't owe me anything, either."

"That's fair enough," she said, surprising him with the simple agreement. "There's nothing wrong with us just traveling on together, for a spell, is there? A man with a woman is less likely to be stopped by a posse than a man traveling alone."

Slocum hesitated. He was good when it came to avoiding posses. Trailwise and clever, the only people always able to track him were Indians. Even then, he knew a trick or two that sometimes put off the best scout. With Glorieta, he would be unable to use many of those tricks.

"They'd be looking at me, not you," she went on. "There aren't many women in these parts, in case you hadn't noticed."

"I noticed," he said. "And I also noticed there's not a one who can hold a candle to you. I think your husband was a damned fool to drag you out here like he did."

"Hans wasn't one who planned carefully," she said without rancor. "But he was a good man." The blue eyes bored into his soul as she added, "Just as you are a good man,

John. The law might be after you, but I see the goodness in you."

Slocum snorted. "You're about the only one."

"Then I'm smarter than the others. You can use that. You're going to rob the Deadwood coach, aren't you? You and that man you were with in the saloon."

"You thinking on helping us out?" Slocum wasn't sure if he was amused or appalled at the idea. Glorieta was a nice woman and not the kind who took part in robberies. He certainly couldn't picture her as a northern version of Belle Starr. For one thing, Glorieta was far prettier than the mud-ugly Belle, and for another she had never crossed the line dividing the law-abiding from the lawless.

"I don't need to stick a six-shooter under someone's nose. I wouldn't know how, even if I can use a rifle fair to middlin' well."

Slocum remembered her accuracy back at the mine. He reckoned she had accounted for more than one Sioux warrior after her family was killed. But it was different robbing a stagecoach than defending yourself from rape and murder.

"I can help you, John, I know it! I can ask questions and find out things you never could."

"Might be," Slocum said. "You don't know what you're getting yourself into, but get your things packed. I want to be in Deadwood inside a couple days."

The deliciously naked Glorieta sprang from bed and embraced him. It took a sight longer leaving Custer City than he had anticipated. And Glorieta was riding beside him on a ten-dollar mule they had bought at the local hostler.

Two days riding due north through the Black Hills got them to the outskirts of Deadwood. It wasn't much different from Custer City, as far as Slocum could see. The plum trees had died back for the season, no longer fed by the two creeks forming the fork near town. Off to one side rose brick houses. Slocum looked at them and shook his head. There was never enough wood in these parts, even though the Black Hills furnished enough for most needs.

Brick and brick factories seemed to make up the financial empires of the prominent citizens in Dakota Territory who hadn't struck it rich with a gold claim.

"There's the ford across the creek," Slocum said after surveying the terrain for several minutes. A crude sign testified that this was Whitewood Creek. Back in August of '75 Frank Bryant had come here looking for gold at the mouth and had named the small stream for the silvery fire-killed trees up the stream a ways. He had spent the winter knee-deep in snow and the following spring had established the Whitewood Mining District.

With any luck, Slocum hoped to be taking some of the gold from Bryant's Discovery Mine when he left Deadwood. From everything he had heard, Bryant would never notice a few pounds missing. He hadn't hit it big. He had hit it *big*.

"Let's go right on through town," Slocum said, coming to a decision. Seth Bullock couldn't have beaten them back to the town, and Slocum wanted a good look at Deadwood before the sheriff returned.

"Is that wise? The sheriff might not be here yet, but he must have left a deputy or two—"

Slocum shook his head. He wasn't even sure Bullock knew him by sight. What would alert any lawman was the presence of a new face in town. He wanted to see how many new faces might be riding through Deadwood on any given day. From the look of the prosperous brick houses and the teeming streets, a drifter might never be noticed. This was a boomtown with all a boomtown's trouble.

"There are so many saloons," Glorieta said softly. "How can there possibly be enough men to fill them?"

"Gold," Slocum said. The entire main street was lined with drinking establishments. He didn't bother telling her most of them were whorehouses, too. From the way men looked at them as they rode by, women were a scarce commodity here.

"We'll find a place to camp. I don't reckon we're likely to find a decent hotel in this place," Slocum said. The few hotels he had seen had No Vacancy signs nailed to their front doors. Men with enough gold dust in their pokes could live there, even with the outrageous rates they likely charged.

"There might be a rooming house," suggested Glorieta.

"Might be," he allowed. He was anxious to find Goodale and get down to work. There was too much gold floating around Deadwood to go untouched for long. The sooner Goodale got his plan in motion, the sooner Slocum could be burdened with the golden weight in his saddlebags.

"John, why don't I look for a place to stay and let you go about your business? We can always meet somewhere. There, for instance." Glorieta pointed to a small restaurant at the junction of the main street and a smaller, quieter one.

"I think you'll be all right," he said. In broad daylight, Glorieta had nothing to fear. After dark was another matter entirely. "Meet you for dinner at six."

"Very well," Glorieta said, but Slocum was already wheeling his horse around and heading back for the center of town. He reined in and stared at the front of a saloon with the simple name No. 10. Something about it wiggled around in his brain just beyond memory.

"This here's the spot where Bill Hickok got shot," a man sitting on the edge of the boardwalk said. "For two bits I'll tell you the whole story. Happened two years ago, August."

"I've heard about it," Slocum said, dismounting.

The man's face fell, then perked up again. "Aces and eights. That's what he was holdin' when he was shot in the back by Crooked Nose Jack McCall. He got himself all tanked up on whiskey. That's the only way he could get the courage to kill the Prince of Pistoleers."

"What happened to McCall?" asked Slocum.

"Judge Kuykendall tried him, right over there at Langrishe's Theatre. Quite a circus it was, too." The man pointed to a melodeon down the street that had seen better days.

"Where'd they hang him?" asked Slocum.

"Didn't. The jury let him go scot-free. A bunch of irate

citizens drug McCall over to Yankton. They hung the son of a bitch there." The man licked his lips and looked up and down the street, as if trying to figure out if he should keep talking or find someone else to badger.

Slocum shrugged and started inside. The man grabbed his arm and said, "They buried Hickok up above Whitewood Creek. Doc Pierce said he was the purtiest corpse he ever laid out. I'll show you the grave for a nickel."

"Here's two bits," Slocum said. "Go find another saloon to spend it in."

The man caught the coin deftly, his head bobbing up and down. "Thank you, sir, thank you, thank you. I got my leg crushed in a mine accident and I can't—"

Slocum spun and went into the saloon. He didn't care about the infamous Deadman's Hand or Hickok. Wild Bill's legend was created by the newspapers, as far as Slocum could tell. The man hadn't killed anywhere near the seventy-five that was claimed. All that counted right now was finding Goodale and seeing to the robbery.

He went to the bar and ordered a beer, wanting something to cut the trail dust in his mouth but not wanting cheap whiskey. He stared straight ahead, not looking around the room in an obvious manner. The dirty, plate glass mirror behind the bar let him do all the scouting he needed. He recognized a half dozen men in the room—all outlaws. One or two might remember him, but he doubted it. He had crossed paths with them and had gone out of his way not to make himself memorable. That was the only way to stay alive.

"You have the look of a man huntin' for a friend," a woman said. A skinny whore sidled up next to him. "You're a handsome one," she said, no expression in her voice. She recited lines she had memorized and couldn't have cared less if he was John Slocum or Wild Bill Hickok's corpse. If he had a small gold nugget or a couple greenbacks to spend, it was all the same to her.

"Might be looking for someone," Slocum said, not turning, "but it's not you. Can't afford it."

"Might be willin' to do it for nuthin'," she said. "A big

strong man like you doesn't come my way every day."

Slocum turned then and studied the room. A door opened at the side of the saloon, leading back to the cribs. If he went through that door with the woman, his stripped corpse would find its way to Whitewood Creek in nothing flat. His six-shooter and clothing would be worth the time it took to lure him away from the main room and kill him.

He reminded himself that Deadwood was a boomtown and *everything* was in short supply. His boots might fetch as much as a hundred dollars, no matter that they were worn and needed repair.

"Goodale," he said suddenly, wanting to see the woman's expression. If she had even heard, she gave no indication. Slocum wasn't sure if this was a good sign or not. Doug Goodale never tried to hide his light under a bushel basket. He came into a town and let everyone know it.

"We can go into the back room. Won't take long. I mean—"

Slocum left most of his beer on the counter and exited the saloon without even looking back at the scrawny woman. The No. 10 bothered him. He had the eerie sensation of ghosts walking through the crowd, bumping elbows, looking over his shoulder. He didn't believe in such nonsense, but there was no denying Wild Bill's spirit remained inside the ill-fated saloon and put a damper on the gaiety. And the ill-kept whore obviously hadn't heard of Goodale. That meant Slocum had to look elsewhere, and do it carefully.

He stepped out into the street, worrying that the begging tour guide would be waiting for him. The man was gone, however. Slocum heaved a sigh of relief for this tiny favor. He wanted to slip through Deadwood without raising any ruckus. The men in the saloon proved to him that more than Doug Goodale intended to make a try at the stagecoach carrying the gold to Cheyenne. If Goodale wasn't going to make his appearance soon, Slocum knew he had to get the information and make a stab at the robbery by himself.

He smiled crookedly as he corrected himself. He wasn't in this alone. Glorieta wanted to be a part of the robbery. Slocum still wasn't sure how this would work out.

Setting off in search of his would-be accomplice, Slocum spent till sundown futilely hunting for Goodale. Tired, just a little bit drunk from all the beer he had been swilling, he turned and went back down the street to the café where Glorieta had agreed to meet him.

He wasn't sure if he was relieved or not when he saw her standing just inside the door. She looked so prim and proper. How was she ever going to fit into a gang of desperadoes waiting to rob the Deadwood stagecoach?

"John!" she said almost breathlessly. "I've been nosing about and have found out a great deal of interest."

"In a minute," he said, taking her by the elbow and guiding her toward an isolated table in the back of the café. Only after they had ordered did he let her continue.

"I've found out a great deal about the shipments and the Gilmer, Saulsbury, and Patrick Stage Company. In July alone, three thousand pounds of quartz was taken to Omaha from the Inter-Ocean Mine. The Wheeler Brothers sent a load of gold dust to the railroad with a guard of twenty men. Other mine owners joined in. By the time it reached the railhead it was a five hundred thousand dollar shipment."

Glorieta paused to suck in air. She was breathless from the recitation. Slocum studied her carefully. He saw the lure of easy money growing in her like a wildfire. A half million dollars was worlds more than her Hans had ever thought to get from the mine with backbreaking twelve-hour-a-day labor.

"How'd you find out all this?" Slocum had to ask. He hadn't been able to find Doug Goodale or anyone who fessed up to knowing him. In fact, he hadn't been able to find out much more than that Deadwood crawled with men capable of any crime. That Glorieta had accumulated so much information in such a short time was nothing less than a miracle.

The dark-haired woman smiled almost shyly and said, "It was easy. I stopped by the Episcopal church."

"What?"

"The Reverend Molyneux is the rector. He's always on the lookout for new members."

"The rector told you all this?" Slocum was amazed.

Glorieta nodded.

Slocum leaned back and laughed. It *was* a miracle.

8

"Move so much as a muscle and I'll plug you, you ugly son of a bitch."

The cold voice came from directly behind Slocum. He paused, his hand twitching slightly. He looked around and gauged his chances for getting out of this without a few ounces of lead slamming through his body. The odds didn't favor him.

"Don't go for it," the voice said.

Slocum stood at the mouth of a long, dark alley. The man was behind him and in the shadows. Even if he succeeded in getting to his Colt Navy and swinging around, he would be dead if the man had the drop on him. Then Slocum relaxed and turned slowly, sure everything was all right.

"You can end up dead pulling damnfool stunts like that, Goodale," he said.

Doug Goodale smiled broadly. "Hasn't killed me yet, Slocum. Don't be such a gloomy Gus. Enjoy life. It's too damn short not to."

"It's too short because people do fool things like sneaking up behind me," Slocum said. He was still on edge and didn't enjoy Goodale's practical joke.

"We got to Deadwood all right, didn't we?" the outlaw said. "Let's go knock back a shot or two and we can discuss what's happening with the robbery. Things are movin' fast, I tell you."

Slocum trailed behind Doug Goodale until they came to the side door of a saloon. Slocum hesitated. To go into a public place was to invite trouble.

"Don't worry, John. This place isn't going to send for Sheriff Bullock. The owner hates the law as much as we do. Come on." Goodale made a sweeping motion with his arm. He laughed at Slocum's reluctance and went inside, whistling "Camptown Races" off-key.

Slocum moved cautiously, his sharp green eyes surveying everyone in the large room. Two whores lounged in the corner, talking to a pair of dusty miners. The miners were in their cups and hardly able to sit upright without the women's willing help. As Slocum watched, one woman slid her hand across the miner's middle, dipped low and gave a squeeze. While this was going on, her left hand was deftly removing the leather pouch tied to his belt by a simple rawhide thong. Slocum snorted. The miner wasn't even going to get kissed.

The others in the saloon looked as if they lived there. A drunk at the far end of the fancy wood bar wobbled. He wasn't a threat. No one could fake being that drunk. The others playing cards never even looked up when Goodale slid a chair back at a far table and sat down.

Goodale waved to Slocum to join him. Still uneasy, Slocum picked up a bottle at the bar. He started to pay for it but the barkeep shook his head and said, "It's on him." He lifted his chin just enough to indicate Goodale.

"Fair enough," said Slocum. He went to the table and set the bottle between them. He hooked a foot around a chair leg and dragged it around until he was able to sit with his back against a wall. Wild Bill Hickok notwithstanding, it never paid to have your back exposed to a room of strangers. Slocum was also able to keep a watch on both the front door and the side entrance he had just used.

"I appreciate your prudence, John, I really do. But it's not necessary. I tell you, nobody in the Northern Empire Saloon is going to run off to fetch the sheriff."

"Reckon not," Slocum said. Their entrance hadn't caused any commotion. The only action in the room was at the table with the four poker players, and they weren't betting more than penny ante.

"Let's get down to business," Goodale said, lowering his voice and hunching forward. He took a shot of the whiskey and sipped at it, making a face. "Terrible hootch. Gimme some of the white lightning like they used to make back home."

"Where's that?" Slocum asked. He knew damned little about Doug Goodale other than what a few days of riding with him had told.

"Back in Tennessee." Goodale finished the shot and poured another. "The stagecoach is going to Cheyenne next week sometime. Rumors have it that it'll leave here on the twenty-sixth and it'll be creaking under its load of gold bullion and dust."

"Whose gold?"

Goodale's eyebrows arched and he looked strangely at Slocum. "What's the difference?"

"Stealing gold from the smaller mines might raise some ruckus, but if we take gold belonging to the larger mines, men with money are going to be pissed."

Goodale smiled crookedly. "They'll be plenty pissed at us. And the U.S. government will, too. There's going to be mail on the coach. Heard tell General Adams from the postal department was out to make sure the U.S. Mail got through without any trouble." Goodale lowered his voice and said, "It's *not* gettin' through to Cheyenne. We'll take it along with the gold."

"Why bother?"

"Money!" he cried. Goodale settled back down. "Men ship greenbacks in the mail. Might take a spell to sit and open all the letters, but we can make another three, four thousand that way. And paper money is easier to carry than specie."

"Not worth the bother," Slocum allowed.

"I'll take care of the mail, then. You can lug off your share in gold dust. We're easy to get along with."

"Who else is in on this?"

"There are a few others, but we got a problem."

Slocum waited for the fly to show up in the pie. He had told himself over and over that it wouldn't be as easy robbing the Deadwood Treasure Coach as Goodale had been making out.

"We need more information about the guards, the driver, the exact route. We need to know more about where the sheriff is likely to be on the twenty-sixth."

"You need to know a damn sight more than that," Slocum said. "If there's a government postal inspector out here, will cavalry be used to escort the stagecoach?"

Goodale shrugged and shook his head. "I don't know. But we can find out."

"How?"

"We need a man on the inside. We need a man like you ridin' with Seth Bullock and givin' us details."

Slocum stared at Goodale in disbelief. "You want me to get hired on as a deputy?"

"Why not? Who'd ever think that a man with your honest face was workin' for a bunch of road agents?"

"This isn't going to work," Slocum said. "Bullock would never hire me as a deputy. I've got a reward on my head. You know that."

"I figured you might, but nobody in Bullock's office cares squat about that. None of them are that bright. You do something to get in his good graces, and by the time anyone notices your face on some smeary wanted poster, we'll have grabbed the gold and be hightailing it for Canada."

"It's only a week till the stagecoach pulls out," Slocum said. "If you got that right."

"If I don't, you can mosey on out, and we'll get the information some other way. All you have to do is ride with the sheriff's men for a week and not one day longer."

"It'd look mighty suspicious if the stagecoach was robbed and then I vanished."

Doug Goodale smiled broadly this time. "Bullock is going to be lookin' for scapegoats everywhere when we pull this off. He's going to look like the world's biggest fool. We're going to steal more gold than a dozen men can carry, right from under his nose. Chances are good that he won't have a deputy left the day after the robbery. They might not be bright, but they're not suicidal. Everyone in Deadwood will be screamin' for their worthless hides."

Slocum considered his position. "What's in it for me?"

"It's dangerous work," Goodale allowed, "and important. Without an inside man we can't be sure the robbery will go smooth. You'd get an equal share."

"Only one share?"

"You're not going to risk getting your balls blowed off like the rest of us," Goodale said.

"I'm just risking having my neck stretched if some eager deputy recognizes me." Slocum worked a bit at his whiskey. "Bullock might even have seen us together back in Custer City."

"He didn't," Goodale said with easy assurance. "He was too busy trying to grab me to pay any attention to anyone with me."

Slocum started to argue a bit more, just from habit rather than any desire to back out of the robbery, when the saloon's swinging doors burst back. Glorieta Zimmermann stood wild-eyed in the doorway. She saw Slocum and made a beeline for him.

"What's—" Slocum didn't get a chance to finish. Glorieta gasped out her warning.

"The sheriff. Seth Bullock. He's down the street with a couple of deputies and he's coming for Mr. Goodale. I overheard them when I was in the clothing store."

"It'll take a few minutes for him to get here," Goodale said. "Howdy do, ma'am." Goodale tipped his hat politely to Glorieta.

"Are you the man John spoke of?"

"I trust he spoke kindly of me," Goodale said. "We're doing a little bit of—business."

"Are you going to join his gang in the stagecoach robbery, John?"

"The sheriff's coming," Slocum said. "We can talk this over somewhere else."

"There's time," insisted Goodale. "I hope John joins in. We want him to side with the sheriff for a spell to provide information on the coach."

"That sounds like a good idea, John. You can do it."

Glorieta's swift agreement dumbfounded him. It was the last thing he had expected from her, but then she had been turning a bit strange. Having her family killed by the Sioux had changed her. Slocum wasn't sure if it was for the best. She was coming to like the danger and promise for immediate wealth offered by a life of thieving. She had yet to realize the danger wasn't a mirage and that she could die a very sudden death if she went along with Goodale's scheme. Men who mined gold didn't take kindly to anyone stealing it.

Slocum couldn't get Mary Surrat from his mind. Secretary of War Stanton had seen to it that the woman was hanged on the flimsiest of evidence after the Lincoln assassination. On the frontier, a posse didn't much care if their victim was a man or a woman. They mostly lusted after spilled blood.

"Why don't you come with me?" suggested Goodale. "That way John'll know exactly where you are."

Slocum said nothing. Goodale wanted the woman as a hostage to insure his cooperation. "It's not necessary," Slocum said. "She can stay here in Deadwood."

"I want to, John. This is exciting. I've never done anything like this before."

"So there," said Goodale.

Slocum glanced out the mud-stained side window and saw the sheriff and three deputies climbing up the steps onto the rickety boardwalk outside the saloon. He whipped out his Colt Navy, kicked back his chair, and yelled at the top of his lungs, "Sheriff Bullock! I got him! I got Doug Goodale here!"

Slocum started firing wildly, smashing bottles behind the bar and driving the barkeep to a spot of safety under the bar. He looked at Goodale. The outlaw tipped his battered brown felt hat in his direction, drew his own six-shooter, and began spraying lead through the front windows. As Goodale fired, he grabbed Glorieta by the elbow and dragged her toward the side door.

Slocum had mixed feelings about Glorieta going with the outlaw. He decided it would work out fine if he played his own role to perfection. He had to convince the sheriff he had tried to stop a known road agent without being recognized.

He emptied his pistol and started reloading. Slocum kept up his loud shouting to make it sound as if a war was going on. By the time the sheriff cautiously poked his head through the front door, Goodale had left with Glorieta.

"He went out that way, sheriff," cried Slocum, pointing out the back. There wasn't any need to lie about it since it was the only way Goodale could have gone. "I tried to take him but couldn't. He's a slippery son of a bitch."

Seth Bullock motioned his three deputies to go after Goodale. He held a smoking pistol with ivory grips in his right hand and locked his left thumb in his gun belt. He advanced, not knowing if he ought to shoot. He came to a conclusion and spit, accurately hitting a brass cuspidor at the end of the bar. The six-shooter stayed in his right hand where he could bring it to bear in a split second.

"Who be you, mister?" Bullock asked Slocum.

"Just a citizen. I recognized Goodale's picture. It was on a wanted poster."

"We heard tell he was here. That's why my men and me came by. Seems you scared the rascal off."

"He was drawing down on me."

Bullock looked Slocum over, starting at the dusty boots and working up the canvas-clad legs. His cold eyes lingered on the worn ebony handle of Slocum's Colt Navy. This was a side arm that had seen considerable use. From the blue shine it had seen use and good care, too. Bullock worked his way higher, past the cross-draw holster until his watery blue eyes locked with Slocum's green ones.

"You a bounty hunter?"

"No." Slocum said it with enough vehemence to convince the sheriff. If there was anything Slocum hated worse in the world than a vigilance committee hot on his trail, it was a bounty hunter.

"Don't take much of a shine to bounty hunters myself. You don't look like a miner, though. Why are you in Deadwood?"

"On my way west," Slocum said.

"Don't plan to stay here?"

"I just want to be on my way. I didn't come here looking for trouble."

"That Doug Goodale anything to you?"

Slocum kept a poker face. "Just another outlaw who ought to be brought to justice."

"You ever worked as a deputy?"

Slocum shrugged and said, "Not exactly. Rode in a posse once or twice."

"I'm needing a half dozen more deputies. If'n you're interested, I might be willing to hire you."

Slocum scratched his chin, pausing long enough to make Bullock think he was considering the pros and cons of the offer. Then he said, "How much does it pay?"

"Not enough," Bullock said. "Not nearly enough. Consider yourself a deputy. We'll get you a badge later. Right now, let's go see if my three hounds have treed that skunk Goodale."

Slocum finished reloading and followed the tall sheriff. Was it really going to be this easy?

9

"The whole of Dakota Territory is in upheaval," Seth Bullock told Slocum. The massive sheriff hitched his thumbs in his belt and leaned forward in the saddle. Slocum worried that the man might fall over with the weight of his worry. The sheriff's black stallion seemed well trained and compensated for the shift in balance on its back and prevented any such toppling. "Ever since that good-for-nothing Bill Hickok got shot two damned years back, everyone's sayin' there's no law in these parts."

"There's no way you could have prevented his killing," Slocum said. He looked around, studying the Black Hills for possible places an ambush could be laid. The rocky ravines were dotted with dozens of spots he would pass along to Doug Goodale.

"That's not the way the good citizens of Deadwood saw it," Bullock said glumly. "They want me to be everywhere all the time. If I bring in one of them for bein' just a tad too drunk, though, then the law's no good and they shout for it to be changed. Damned if I do and damned if I don't."

They rode slowly along the Cut-Off Trail, retracing the path Slocum had taken just two days earlier. He couldn't keep his eyes off the unmarked mounds along the trail. Too many men had died here and been laid to rest in unmarked graves. If he got the information from the sheriff that Goodale wanted, he might insure that he and Goodale and the others getting ready to rob the coach wouldn't be planted here, too.

"This here is Red Canyon," Bullock said. "There's been eleven stagecoach robberies along this stretch in the past month. The road agents just don't give us a rest."

"The hills are producing a heap of gold. That's a mighty big lure for the lawless," Slocum said. He had to work hard to keep his own face neutral as he spoke. The lure of such wealth made his heart race just a mite faster. Soon enough he would have his share of it and be on his way to Canada.

"Why are you showing me all this?" Slocum asked suddenly. "There's a considerable amount of work to be done just in Deadwood."

Bullock laughed harshly. "Those eleven robberies are creatin' quite a stir among the very men who pay our salaries, such as they are. Bryant is screamin' bloody murder. So are a couple other big mine owners. If we don't put a stop to the robberies soon, we'll be out of jobs. It don't matter much about a few drunks shooting up the town. The gold robberies are what have to be stopped."

Slocum hardly considered the loss of a job paying only twenty-five dollars a month worth losing sleep over. Even worse, the salary came in greenbacks. There wasn't a saloon in Deadwood that didn't discount the paper money by at least a quarter before giving a decent drink. The treasure coach offered the chance for real money and more than he could make as a deputy in a hundred years.

"Going out on the twenty-sixth?" Slocum asked. "The big gold shipment on the stagecoach?"

Bullock turned and shot a hard look at him. "Where'd you hear that?"

Slocum tried to keep expressionless as he said, "That's what they're saying in the bars. Is it wrong?"

"The date's right," grumbled Bullock. "How the hell am I supposed to guard the damned thing when every outlaw in Dakota Territory knows when it's leaving?"

"You can change the date and fool them," Slocum suggested.

Bullock snorted in contempt. His breath came out in silvery plumes as the autumn air turned colder and colder. There wasn't any chance that the sheriff could change the shipment. The owners of the mines had decreed that the gold had to get to Cheyenne. Tinkering with their plan now would only cause more trouble than it was worth.

Slocum reined in and pointed. "Sheriff? See that spot ahead? Looks as if someone's been camping there recently."

"So?"

"So there's no reason for them not to come on into Deadwood. Why stay here?" Slocum rode over to the campsite and dismounted. "More'n a dozen men, unless I miss my guess," he said. Slocum walked around, poking at the campfire ashes with his toe. "They stayed here for a day or more. The fire's a big one, even for that many men."

"You're saying this was a bunch of road agents?"

"Could have been," Slocum said. His mind raced. He didn't think Goodale would be stupid enough to camp this close to the trail where the stagecoach would roll in just a few days. This had to be the spoor of another gang—and another gang might have the same dreams of robbing the Deadwood Treasure Coach.

"Took off into the hills," Bullock said, squinting at the trail left by the riders. "Not more'n a day old. Less."

"Should we follow?"

"Damnation, man, we can't take on a dozen armed men by ourselves. Even Jack Crawford's vigilantes over in Custer City wouldn't stand much of a chance going after them."

"You're just going to let them go on their way?" Slocum put enough sarcasm into the question to rile the sheriff a mite. He wanted to get the lawman het up and on the trail of other outlaws. That opened the way for Goodale when the treasure-laden stagecoach rolled out of its Deadwood depot.

"Let's keep riding. I want to show you the rest of the way

down to Jenny's Stockade. After it leaves there, it's out of my jurisdiction. Let the damned cavalry worry about it on into Cheyenne."

They rode in silence. Slocum kept a keen eye out for other possible ambush points. The one where the men had camped looked to be the best—or so Slocum thought until they got to a level area that gradually tailed off to a small oasis in the middle of the desolate hills.

"That there's Cold Springs," Bullock said. "The driver changes horses for the first time—all six of them. From here the land gets rocky and the going is harder."

Slocum saw the road rise up and vanish in a serpentine of twisting rocky trail hardly worth the name. This was the perfect spot for the robbery. The driver would be coasting here. His team would be exhausted from the rough going along the Cut-Off Trail. He couldn't turn and run, he could hardly continue on if the outlaws were waiting at Cold Springs, and most of all, the driver would be lulled into thinking he had just come safely through an area where eleven other robberies had been committed.

Cold Springs. The name filled Slocum with a warmth that bespoke of glittering gold.

"Are there any guards at the changeover station?" Slocum asked. He saw no indication that the small stables or log house were fortified.

"No need. The driver seldom gets this far unscathed."

"Won't on next Tuesday, either," Slocum said. "That gang will be waiting to pluck the gold from the stagecoach just as sweet as you please."

Seth Bullock grumbled under his breath, then said just loud enough for Slocum to hear, "Damn me if you're not right. We can wait till nightfall. Josh and the others will show up by then. We can go after those bastards in a couple days and dig them out of their hideout all proper-like. This time the stagecoach is going through untouched or my name's not Seth Bullock!"

Slocum smiled as he rode alongside the earnest lawman. This was working out better than either he or Doug Goodale could have hoped. He had the date on the stagecoach's departure. He had found the perfect spot for the stickup. He knew at least one other group he could get the sheriff to chase and eliminate.

Slocum grinned. Doug Goodale's plan was working out better than he had thought. Slocum was about ready to start counting his share of the take from the robbery.

"The bastards are up there in the rocks," Seth Bullock said glumly. The man's gloomy forecast echoed down through the ranks of the small posse he had assembled. Digging even a few men out of that rocky fortress would take an entire cavalry company.

"I can scout them out," said Slocum. "If we know where they are, we might be able to sneak up on them."

"You can do that without them seein' you?" Bullock shook his head. "Not even a Sioux warrior could get up there without a blind sentry spotting him."

"Won't hurt to try," said Slocum. He was getting itchy riding with the other deputies. One named Lowry kept staring at him, as if he was trying to puzzle out where he had seen Slocum before. When it occurred to the lawman to start digging through old wanted posters, Slocum intended to be far away and spending some of the gold from the stagecoach robbery.

At the moment, he was just happy to put some distance between him and the rest of the posse. He wasn't cut out to be a deputy.

"Go on. We'll give you a couple hours. Reckon the boys won't mind a little rest." Bullock looked over his shoulder and saw relief flooding the expressions of his men. They had ridden hard all morning and hadn't come up with squat in the way of outlaws. To have to fight now, tired and hungry, meant more of them would get killed. Better to rest up and let the newcomer get killed on a harebrained manhunt.

Slocum heaved a sigh of relief as the others dismounted and started a small cooking fire to fix coffee and heat beans. He urged his faithful sorrel up the steep, rocky slope and let her pick her way. When he was out of sight of the sheriff's posse, Slocum dismounted and led the horse to give her a much needed rest. He didn't know if he could locate the outlaw gang that he and the sheriff had found two days earlier, but he didn't think it would be too difficult. When he did, he wanted his horse rested and ready to ride.

Slocum found a quiet spot and sat down. He pulled out some jerky and began gnawing at it. He spat a few times to get the maggots out, then leaned back and stared at the azure sky as he contentedly chewed. This holdup was working out well so far. Doug Goodale wasn't doing his usual reckless robbery. He was showing real caution and careful planning. Slocum didn't feel right wearing the tin badge on his vest, but he'd get over it. Enough gold always made things right.

He heaved himself to his feet and began a careful search of the terrain. When he found rocks that had been chipped and scratched by shod horses, he knew he was on the right track. The cuts were still shiny and sharp, showing the outlaw band had passed this way only a day or two earlier. That jibed well with his notion that these were the men who had camped down by the Cut-Off Trail. Slocum spent the next couple of hours working his way back and forth across the rocky slopes, moving ever higher. He stared up into the hills and decided he knew where the outlaw company had their camp.

Sniffing hard, he caught the scent of a fire. Someone had fixed a noonday meal, and they weren't far away.

Tethering his horse, he went ahead on foot. Slocum kept a sharp lookout for sentries. He almost stumbled into the camp by accident. The road agents hadn't even bothered to post guards. They thought they were secure in their hilly hideaway.

He dropped to his belly and pulled out the folding brass telescope. Slocum checked to be sure there wouldn't be any revealing glints off the shiny tube to warn the men assembled in the draw below, then he began studying the area. They had chosen well, but without sentries, they were sitting ducks.

Counting slowly, he got to nine and ran out of men and horses for them. He couldn't determine what weapons they had with them, but he doubted there was anything more than a few rifles and side arms. Slocum lifted the end of his spyglass and worked around the ravine, finding several possible ways of attacking. Satisfied with his reconnaissance, he collapsed the telescope, put it back into its carrying case, and rolled onto his back. It would take the better part of two hours getting back to where Bullock had camped. From there, if the sheriff decided to take these outlaws, it would be another two hours to attack. By then it would be twilight.

Slocum thought this was perfect for an attack.

He hurried back to his horse. He had things to report to the sheriff.

"Yep, it's exactly as you laid out," said Bullock, almost in awe. "This is going to be easier than using a keg of blasting powder on a baby. We split up—"

"Sheriff, is that smart?" asked the deputy who kept giving Slocum the hard looks. "If we split up, that weakens our attack."

"It cuts off their retreat, you dunderhead," snapped Bullock. "Any fool can see that. We want them for trial, not to get away. Sometimes I don't think you got good sense, Lowry."

"There are only the two good ways in and out of the draw," Slocum said, scratching a crude map in the thin dirt. "We cut them off and they'll give up. Either that or we cut them down where they stand."

"You make it sound easy. It ain't gonna be," Lowry said, still glaring at Slocum. "This is probably the Bill Bivens gang. They're cold-blooded killers."

"Then it's a good thing we have them trapped, isn't it?" Slocum said in a wintry voice. "The sheriff's right. This is a good plan."

"Lowry," the sheriff said to the deputy, "you take four of the men and go to the far cut in the hills. We'll drive them toward you, those that don't give up outright."

"This way you don't have to even draw your six-shooter," Slocum said in a nasty tone. He didn't want to bait Lowry, but he couldn't help himself. The man was acting like a coward and Slocum hated that.

Lowry started for his pistol, but Bullock moved faster. His thick-fingered hand grabbed his deputy's wrist and squeezed down hard. Lowry's face turned pale, but the anger remained.

"Let's keep this for the outlaws," Bullock said. "You got your orders. Take off, Lowry. Now!"

Slocum watched the deputy leave, knowing he had made a mistake. Lowry wouldn't quit until he either shot Slocum in the back or rooted through the wanted posters and had something to show the sheriff. He had eyed Slocum too long not to be just a tad suspicious of the new deputy.

"Glad to have you in my employ," Bullock said to Slocum, "but don't go rilin' him none. He's a mean one, and he's got a hair-trigger temper. I'm thinking we are going to need all the guns we can muster, leastwise until after the coach is on its way and past Jenny's Stockade going on to Fort Laramie."

"Out of the Deadwood jurisdiction," Slocum said. He checked his Colt Navy, found it was in perfect working condition, and slid it back into his cross-draw holster. He was ready, even if he didn't much want to go up against the road agents holed up in the ravine.

They rode in silence until they reached the point where Slocum indicated they ought to dismount. He didn't want to chance them blundering onto a newly posted sentry. Bullock made a gesture and the four men with him dismounted. Slocum advanced, carefully picking his way up the rocky slope. The sun was setting behind the Black Hills and cast elongated shadows in front of him. He was especially careful not to give away his position by standing too tall. The long shadow would alert anyone even halfway awake.

"There they are," Slocum said. Two cooking fires blazed merrily. The nine men lounged about, not a care in the world. That would change in the next few minutes.

"I reckon Lowry ought to be in position in the far draw in another ten minutes. Let's wait a spell and see if he signals us." Bullock leaned back and pulled out a bag of fixings. He started to roll a cigarette, then thought better of it. There wasn't much of a breeze blowing this evening. Even a whiff of tobacco smoke might alarm the highwaymen below.

"There," said Slocum after they had waited almost fifteen minutes. "That's Lowry. He's in position to block off their retreat."

Bullock squinted. "Must be. Either that or the young fool's decided to get out his mirror and shave that fuzzy chin of his." Bullock had positioned the others immediately after they had arrived. All had good posts to fire down into the draw. The outlaws wouldn't stand a chance if they chose to fight it out.

"Let's do it." Bullock heaved himself up and stood outlined against the setting sun. "You men down there, this here's Seth Bullock, sheriff over in Deadwood. I'm arresting the lot of you for robbery."

The hail of bullets didn't faze the sheriff. He stood his ground. A gesture to his right and three men opened fire. Another brought rifle fire from the remaining deputy. Slocum stayed hunkered down beside the sheriff, staring in amazement at his foolhardy stance.

"Don't get such an expression on your face, boy," he told Slocum. "There's no way they can hit me from down there. They'd be firing uphill, always a hard shot, and all they got is six-shooters. I'm out of range, but does it ever make me look like a hero in my deputies' eyes."

Slocum stayed down. The slug from a .44 carried quite a distance. Here and there around him he heard the sharp *ping!* of ricochets. The outlaws below might not be able to fire accurately, but their bullets were getting up the slope. A poorly aimed bullet was as likely to snatch a man's life as a well aimed one in a fight like this.

"There they go," said Bullock. "Six of them are tryin' to get past Lowry. Let's see if the young buck is up to stopping them."

Slocum slid around the boulder he had used for protection and peered into the gathering gloom of the draw. Two men stood with their hands held high. A third lay sprawled on his back in the dust. The other six had hightailed it to their horses, thinking they could escape.

The fusillade coming from the distant ravine told of Lowry's deadly accuracy. None of the six got free.

"He'll be the death of me. I wanted them for trial," Bullock said when it became apparent all six who had fled were now drawing flies. Lowry and his men had cut them down as they rode out, not giving them a chance to surrender.

"Saves the taxpayers the cost of a trial," spoke up another deputy.

"That's not the point," said Bullock. "I reckon these owlhoots were going to make an attempt on the treasure coach. With them in jail, everyone could see what a damn good job I'm doing. Now—" His voice trailed off.

Slocum mentally finished the sentence for the sheriff. "Now all I got are new graves in the Whitewood Cemetery."

Slocum vowed not to be another addition in the Deadwood potter's field.

10

The Bill Bivens gang—what there was left of them—were safely locked up in the Deadwood jail. Sheriff Bullock had received a fair amount of accolades for the capture, but privately he still cursed his deputy, Lowry, for being a trigger-happy fool. Slocum kept in the background as much as possible. The wild light in Lowry's eyes told him the deputy was turning kill-crazy. He had seen it before in other men, and he didn't like it.

The ways of dealing with a mad-dog killer were simple. Either get away from him or shoot him down before he killed you. Neither path was open to Slocum. He had to stick around Deadwood long enough to find out what he could about the treasure coach. The Gilmer, Saulsbury, and Patrick Stage Company was preparing it for departure in a couple of days. He knew it wasn't quite ready yet because the stationmaster had called Sheriff Bullock over to inspect it several times in the past few hours. Each time there had been something lacking.

Slocum considered robbing the bank where the gold was kept before it was loaded onto the coach. When he saw the cavalry troopers milling about the bank, he knew it could never work that way. The stagecoach had to be robbed without the soldiers' protection.

"See you lookin' at the bluecoats," Bullock said. Slocum tried not to jump, but the sheriff had startled him. He vowed not to let himself get so caught up in his own thoughts.

"Reckon I was," Slocum allowed. "Are they going to guard the coach when it leaves day after tomorrow?"

"They're just lookin' after their payroll."

"A military payroll's going to be on the stagecoach?" This took Slocum by surprise. He was willing to let Doug Goodale have the U.S. Mail that would be loaded on, but a government payroll, too? This might get the wrong folks riled. He reckoned as to how he could run far enough so that the mine owners would never catch him. Robbing a few pieces of mail might get that General Adams upset, but it wasn't going to be anything that would follow a man for long.

Stealing a cavalry payroll, however, was something else. The bluecoats never forgot. Government theft was damned near as bad as judge-killing, which Slocum had learned about the hard way.

Was robbing a government payroll worth even more posters?

He almost laughed at the idea. They couldn't hang him but once. Better to have the entire cavalry chasing a rich robber than end up poor and in some ramshackle jail waiting to be hanged on the charge of killing a no-account federal judge.

"This is going to be one of the best protected shipments ever," said Bullock. "The cavalry's decided to entrust the Fort Cheyenne pay to it. And why not? We wiped out the Bivens gang. There're enough others out there willing to try to rob the stagecoach, but after we bring Bivens to trial tomorrow, that might make them think twice."

"He's being tried so soon?"

"Might as well try him now. The circuit judge is in town for a week or more. No sense postponin' the obvious. The sooner we try Bivens, the sooner we can send him to prison."

"That'll make the others sit up and take notice, yes sir," Slocum said. He spoke now just to make conversation. His mind raced. The threat of a trial might make a few of the many gangs of road agents working the Cut-Off Trail take a powder. That eliminated competition for the treasure coach robbery, and he liked the notion. But the really hard-boiled outlaws wouldn't care.

Doug Goodale would still have some competition for this fabulous shipment.

Slocum had found out as much about the heavily laden coach as he could. He slipped out of town and rode steadily into the Black Hills until he was sure no one followed him. He circled around, checking to see if he might have made a mistake. He didn't trust Lowry. For all the wild-eyed posturing the deputy did, he was a competent enough lawman and not one to cross without knowing the odds.

He sat astride the sorrel for almost a half hour before deciding that the only people moving down the trail were going into Deadwood. Slocum wheeled the horse and trotted off, hunting for the spot where Doug Goodale had promised he would be camped. Slocum was anxious to see the caliber of men the outlaw had recruited for the robbery. It wouldn't be easy going, even with the best men in the Black Hills.

If Slocum was risking his neck pretending to be a deputy, Goodale had better be keeping up his end of the robbery. There wasn't much time before that gold-heavy stagecoach rolled out on its way to Cheyenne. Any change in plans now would likely mean the robbery had to be called off. The notion of spending a week as deputy and then getting nothing for it would rankle.

Slocum rode slowly, his keen eyes peeled for any sign that Goodale had been in the area. He saw nothing. He rode farther along the Cut-Off Trail and deeper into Red Canyon. The more he rode, the edgier he got. He didn't see any sign of Goodale. Just when he was beginning to think the outlaw had taken it into his head to leave the Dakota Territory, he heard the sound of horses. Slocum reined back and listened carefully. He turned slightly and homed in on the distinctive whinnies of horses being fed.

A small canyon looked like the best chance he had of

finding the camp. Slocum dismounted and walked his sorrel. When he caught a whiff from a campfire, he tethered the horse and advanced on foot. He dropped to his belly when he saw the glint of sunlight off a carelessly held rifle barrel. A bearded man in a red-checked shirt sat atop a large rock, his rifle balanced across his lap, as he worked on rolling a cigarette. Slocum slipped past the sentry without being seen.

Doug Goodale's camp consisted of a small lean-to and four bedrolls scattered over the rocky slope of a hill.

"Glorieta gets the lean-to," came a quiet voice. "Ain't much, but it is better than sleeping under the stars."

"Didn't think I was going to find you," Slocum said, relaxing slightly. "And you're still trying to sneak up on me. You're going to get ventilated if you keep doing that."

"Hasn't affected me adversely yet," said Doug Goodale, coming down from a perch on a boulder. "You're too good to turn and plug me, John. You got reflexes like a snake and you've got a brain. You're always considerin' this and that. You knew this was my camp. You knew it was me up on the rock."

"I know that's a piss-poor lookout you've got back down the trail."

"Old Ben used to be a miner. This is still a bit new for him. Best powder monkey in the Black Hills, though."

"Why do you want a miner in on this?"

"Come on into camp, John. We got a mite to talk over. I want to hear all about your foray into Deadwood." Goodale tapped the battered badge hanging on Slocum's vest. "This looks real peculiar on you. Truly, it does."

"You only got three others?" Slocum searched the camp for some sign that Goodale had more men posted around. He saw no evidence of it. The horses in the makeshift corral didn't seem the least bit lonely for others of their kind.

"This is it. The fewer we take along for the ride, the more we each get. Makes sense, doesn't it, John?"

"It makes sense that we're going to need a small army and five of us isn't anywhere near enough. Especially if the others are like that miner on sentry duty."

"The other two are all right. Reckon you might have heard of them. Here they come now. They've been with Glorieta fetching water. The nearest stream is about a hundred yards over the ridge."

Slocum saw the three make their way carefully down the slope. The men carried buckets and Glorieta looked more radiant than ever. Slocum wondered if she intended to go through with the robbery to the bitter end or if she would come to her senses and decide to go home to Chicago. As much as he enjoyed the nights he'd spent with her, he wanted her out of his hair. This was a dangerous game he and Goodale played. They knew the risks; she didn't. To her this robbery was little more than a spot of excitement in an otherwise directionless life.

"That there on Glorieta's left is McLaughlin. He rode with Frank and Jesse James for a spell before coming north to try his luck. And the other one's Rod Ker—"

Doug Goodale didn't get to finish the introduction. When the second man saw Slocum, he went for his pistol. Slocum was faster. His hand closed on the ebony handle of his Colt Navy, drew and cocked and got off the first shot. It was good enough. The man sank to the ground as if someone had turned his legs to mush.

"What's all that about?" Goodale asked, his own hand resting on his six-shooter.

"He was with the Bill Bivens gang," Slocum said. "Sheriff Bullock rousted them a few days back. The only way he could have gotten out of jail was to strike a deal."

"Hell's bells," grumbled Goodale. "I thought he was a mite anxious to join up, even when he didn't know what we were planning."

"You mean he would have turned us all over to the sheriff?" Glorieta Zimmermann stared at the dead outlaw, her face as pale as bleached muslin.

"There was probably a considerable reward attached to the offer," Slocum said. He worried that the sheriff hadn't seen fit to tell him about the double-crossing outlaw. That meant the sheriff suspected him of being something more than just another deputy.

"But I—he—oh!" Glorieta buried her face in her hands and turned and rushed off.

Doug Goodale's hand closed on Slocum's shoulder when he tried to follow her. "Let her bawl a mite. The cry will do her good."

"What was he to her?" Slocum asked.

"Let's not go gettin' personal in this. We've been camped here for damned near a week. A man gets lonely." Goodale cleared his throat. "A woman does, too."

Slocum went cold inside. He had thought he meant more to Glorieta. He had been wrong.

"The coach is going to carry an army payroll," Slocum said, changing the subject. His eyes kept wandering, trying to follow Glorieta. He forced them back to Goodale.

"So much the better," Goodale said, gloating. "I can just feel those greenbacks sliding over my fingers now. The paper spends damn near as good as the gold."

"There might be a cavalry company going along. We could never get it if there is."

"There *might* be? Is there going to be an armed escort or not, John?"

"Bullock is hoping he's jailed all the owlhoots eager to get a piece of the gold," Slocum admitted. "He and I rode over the entire route through Red Canyon, all the way to Jenny's Stockade."

"So? Where's the best spot for our ambush?"

Slocum related all he had seen about Cold Springs. The tired team, the promise of rest for the driver and guards, and the terrain would all go a long way toward making the robbery go down quick and painless there.

"Sounds like the perfect spot. But something's eatin' at you. What is it, John?"

"That one." Slocum pointed at the man he had just gunned down. "Bullock let him out of jail and didn't tell me. He and the sheriff had made some kind of deal."

"So?"

"So if the sheriff didn't trust me enough to tell me he was letting that one go, why'd he trust me enough to ride down the Cut-Off Trail and point out all the spots where eleven prior robberies had been? It doesn't make sense."

"Sheriff Bullock might just be a cautious sort," Goodale said. "There's no need for him to go spillin' his guts to every new deputy about every little thing he does. You done good roundin' up the Bivens gang. He must have been impressed a mite on account of that."

"We did ride out to Cold Springs just after you and Glorieta hightailed it."

"That was a mighty fine piece of acting," said Goodale. "If you hadn't been spraying the lead around so wild, I'd've thought you meant it."

"I don't miss when I aim," Slocum said coldly.

Doug Goodale glanced toward the fallen man and nodded. "I do think that is the gospel truth."

Slocum hunkered down and poured himself a cup of coffee. He couldn't keep his mind on the matter at hand. He kept thinking about Glorieta. He ought to find her and have it out, but business pressed in on him. It wouldn't be much longer before he had to return to town. If a deputy vanished two days before the richest stagecoach in Deadwood history rolled out, Seth Bullock would smell a rat.

"So who are you going to get to replace him?"

Goodale shrugged. "Can't say I gave it much thought. We might be able to get by with McLaughlin, the miner, and me—and you and Glorieta, of course."

"She's not taking part in this." Slocum's words were cold, harsh.

Goodale shook his head. "That's not the way she's tellin' it. She *wants* to be a part of it. A pistol-totin' part. With Kerwin out of it, there's no time to recruit anyone else. I got to tell her she's in, if she still wants."

"She's out," Slocum said.

Goodale stared at him, a sly smile twisting his lips. He started to speak, then ended with a broad grin that Slocum didn't like. The notion of robbing the Deadwood Treasure Coach appealed to him. How the robbery was progressing didn't. The army payroll meant a closer watch might be kept on the stagecoach. Slocum didn't think the cavalry company would accompany the coach, but he didn't know. If they did, the robbery was off. Three men and a woman stood no chance at all against trained troopers.

Even with just the Gilmer, Saulsbury, and Patrick Stage Company guards, it was a prodigious job with high risk. Knowing something of the details made it easier—but not enough.

"Just you, McLaughlin, and the miner?"

"Well, John, that's what it's got to be unless you can ride out of town and join us. Or better, can you get yourself assigned as a guard? That would make the heist go even better."

"Bullock hasn't said anything about sending a deputy from Deadwood. He wouldn't send one all the way to Cheyenne, no matter what."

"That's fine. If'n you just went as far as Cold Springs, we'd be happier than pigs in a wallow."

Slocum considered this. He hadn't thought much about Bullock's responsibility. He might be able to talk the sheriff into accompanying the stagecoach, if Bullock didn't suspect him. With the dead outlaw from the Bivens gang spying on Goodale, that meant the sheriff knew others intended to rob the stagecoach.

Slocum snorted. Only a fool would think that stopping one gang would prevent an attempt on the coach. The entire Dakota Territory was crawling with road agents.

"I'll look into it. If I can't arrange it, where do we meet after the robbery to split the take?"

"Well, John," said Goodale, his words evenly spaced and his tone low, "there's a spot down near Custer City that is just about perfect. It's off the Cut-Off Trail in a little canyon with tiny piles of red stones stacked on either side of the entrance. They look like bedposts, you know the kind. If we meet there, we could divvy up and go our separate ways."

Slocum stopped looking at Doug Goodale and started listening hard to the way he spoke. The man's measured tones sounded like he was reciting a school lesson. That could only mean he had been going over this time and again—and he was lying through his teeth.

"Will you have spare horses there?" Slocum asked.

Goodale looked surprised at this. "A good idea. I hadn't thought on it. I'll have McLaughlin go rustle a couple spares for each of us. If either the cavalry or Bullock—or even that crazy Jack Crawford from Custer City—come after us, it'd be a good idea to have spares to swap off now and again."

"We'll need packhorses for the gold, too. There's going to be a mountain of bullion."

"That's why I favor the greenbacks to the specie," Goodale said with some relish. "They don't spend as good, but you can carry tons of them." He laughed and poured himself some coffee.

Slocum got more from the pot, then settled down to think real hard. If Doug Goodale planned a double-cross, how could Slocum turn this to his benefit? He couldn't rely on Glorieta to help him.

Or could he? With the sheriff's spy dead, Glorieta might be more inclined to throw in with him again than with Goodale. Slocum needed information. The Cold Springs way station was the only place where the robbery could succeed. Doug Goodale had to strike there.

But where would he go when he had the gold? How much could Slocum trust him? Those were questions only Glorieta could answer for him.

11

Slocum tossed the dregs of his coffee into the campfire. A loud hiss sounded and sent a thin column of steam wisping into the air. He dropped the tin cup and stood.

"You goin' back so soon, John?" Doug Goodale looked at him from half-hooded eyes. Slocum knew then that it was a lead pipe cinch the outlaw was going to double-cross him. That was the only possible reason for his sleepy look. He wanted to keep his eyes from betraying his intentions to Slocum.

"Not just yet. I want to talk a spell with McLaughlin and find out what that miner you got stuck up on the rock can really do. Then I might talk to the miner himself."

"Don't go bothering the poor man. He's not too bright." Goodale tapped the side of his head to indicate the miner was a trifle on the feebleminded side. "He's a good man, though. He'll do what has to be done. Me and McLaughlin will do the bulk of the work."

"And Glorieta," Slocum said.

"No, not her. You said to deal her out of the game. I'm not goin' against the wishes of my inside man. You're the key player in this game, John, yes sir. We need you. Nobody can do what you're doin' in town. It's a big risk playing the deputy like you are, and I surely do appreciate that. We need the information you're bringin' back to us about the stagecoach."

The praise struck Slocum as fulsome. Goodale didn't have to slather on the words like this. It made Slocum even more certain there was going to be a double-cross.

"I'll leave him be. I do want to talk to McLaughlin. Any problem with that?"

"None, John. You got a right to know how we're settin' things up out here. McLaughlin will get those horses and have them waiting in the canyon." Goodale's words didn't ring true—or there was something he wasn't telling.

"You don't sound too sure of this," Slocum said. "You hatching out a better plan?"

"Might be," Goodale said, as if coming to a huge decision. "Set yourself back down for a minute and let me see how this strikes you." Goodale pointed to a rock near the small fire. He seemed to be composing himself for still another round of lying. "We've been thinking in terms of gettin' the gold out of Dakota Territory straightaway after the robbery. Maybe that's not the way to go about it."

Slocum said nothing. He wanted to hear what Goodale really had on his mind, but he didn't think the outlaw would get that far. This was still part of the double-cross.

"That gold's heavy. Look at the preparations they're making to transport it. The stagecoach is a special Concord, made to carry several hundred pounds of metal, in addition to the passengers, their luggage, a few bags of mail."

"So?"

"So we'll need *pack* mules to get it out. You mentionin' packhorses plus riding spares brought this to mind. We can't hope to skip ahead of a righteously determined posse, not if everything I've heard about Bullock is true."

"He's an honest man," allowed Slocum. "He's been pushed to the wall by the robberies, and I don't think he'd give up easily when we've robbed the coach."

"My point exactly," said Goodale, warming to his talk. He leaned forward just enough, though, to keep his eyes hidden. Slocum remembered that Goodale never was a good poker player. For all the passion in the man's words,

Slocum still thought it sounded rehearsed, as if Goodale had gone over it carefully in his head to be sure Slocum swallowed it hook, line, and sinker. Slocum slowly realized the outlaw would never have started on this new lie if he hadn't been adamant about talking to McLaughlin and Glorieta before returning to Deadwood. This might be a second step in a double-cross. Slocum knew he had to proceed carefully and look as if he believed everything or Goodale might just try to shoot him in the back as he rode out.

Good sense dictated that he ride out of camp and just keep going, but greed was nudging him with a golden elbow. The take from the treasure coach was too rich to walk away from without making some effort and taking some risk.

"What if we didn't cart off the gold at all?" Goodale went on. "What if we cached it and then got our asses out of the territory? We could sneak back in come next spring and waltz on out without the sheriff breathin' down our necks. Who'd look for us in, say, six months?"

"That's a much better idea than trying to dodge a posse," Slocum agreed. "I didn't cotton much to having to lug that much gold along with me as I rode to Canada. So you're saying we should hide it, then come back and fetch it all later?"

"Why not? We got the powder monkey out there. He's an expert at blasting. We can stash the gold in an old mine, blow the shaft, and then dig it out next year. It wouldn't be the work of a minute for him to rig a charge to hide the gold."

"The idea appeals to me," said Slocum. "What about the greenbacks?"

Doug Goodale laughed heartily. "Never could fool you for a minute, could I, John? All right, we split that right away. But we come back for the gold."

"What's to keep one of us from coming back early and taking all the gold?" Slocum had to ask the obvious question even though it was pointless. If he hadn't, Goodale would have known he hadn't pulled the wool over his eyes.

"That's the beauty of it. That's why we bury it in an old mine shaft. It'll take several weeks to dig it out. There's no way any of us could do it alone in winter. It gets damned cold here in the Black Hills. We have a few weeks of backbreaking labor ahead of us come spring, but the take will be worth it, won't it? Won't there be enough gold to make us all rich?"

"There will. Everything I've heard says there is going to be a couple hundred pounds of gold aboard the stagecoach. Maybe more." Slocum knew this trick, too. Goodale wanted him thinking of how much he could make in the robbery rather than the details that didn't ring true. There wouldn't be any mine shaft. There wouldn't be anyone coming back in the spring. Slocum wasn't even sure if McLaughlin and the powder monkey were being dealt into Goodale's hand.

And what about Glorieta Zimmermann? Where did she fit into the puzzle of Goodale's plans for the gold?

"We're going to be rich," Slocum said, playing the game, too. "How you going to spend your split?"

"Haven't thought much about it." If there hadn't been anything else Goodale had said that sparked caution in Slocum, this was it. Every robber thought exactly about what he'd do with such a hoard of gold. "Reckon there's a spread waitin' for someone like me. Maybe down in Texas. Raisin' longhorns is real profitable, and I can see myself owning a few thousand acres."

Slocum almost laughed. Doug Goodale wasn't the settling-down, ranching type. He had been born to steal, and he would die doing it. Whether he swung with a rope around his neck or got shot during a holdup, he was a thief through and through. No cattle ranch, regardless of its size, could hold his interest for very long.

Slocum pulled out his brother Robert's watch and popped open the case. He studied the dial for a spell, then snapped it shut. "I don't have much time before I get on back to Deadwood. I don't reckon there's any need to talk with McLaughlin. He seems like a steady customer. But I do want to talk to Glorieta before I go."

"Might be a good idea," said Goodale. "She's not going to take kindly to the way you cut down Kerwin."

Slocum left the outlaw lounging beside the fire. He had

no trouble following the trail left by Glorieta as she fled into the hills. Here and there he saw bushes with bits of her dress stuck to the thorns. She had run without regard to the damage done to her clothing.

He found her sitting on top of the rise, forehead down on her raised knees. She looked up, her blue eyes filled with tears. Slocum paused, not knowing what her reaction would be. If Rod Kerwin had been her lover, she might not want to speak with him right now.

Again she surprised him. "I'm glad you came up here, John," she said. "I'm so ashamed!" She began crying, her entire body quaking with the power of her emotions.

"About what?" Slocum asked. He hadn't decided where Glorieta fit into the double-cross Goodale was so obviously planning. She might be in the dark. He hoped so, but he wasn't counting on it. She had changed too much from the honest woman he had known ever so briefly after her family was killed.

"I—he— Oh, John! I let him make love to me! He was an animal!"

"Kerwin? He was arrested a few days back with a couple others from the Bill Bivens gang. The sheriff must have made a deal with him to spy on us."

"I had never met anyone like him. He was a silver-tongued fox. He made me feel—different." She looked up, tears spilling from her sapphire eyes. "I wish you hadn't gone into town. I wish you hadn't left me. I don't have any experience with men like that. Don't leave me again, John. Please. Promise. Promise!"

He found himself holding her shaking body and trying to comfort her. At this moment it was damned hard to believe she was going to try to steal his share of the gold from the robbery.

"I've got to get back to town soon," he said, still undecided about her intentions. "If I don't, Bullock will get suspicious. He'll put so many men to guarding the stage-coach we'll never be able to rob it."

"Forget the coach. Let's just leave."

"We've got to try. Tell me what you can about Goodale's

plan. He and I didn't have time to discuss much of it."

Slocum waited.

What he heard chilled him.

"Doug said we got to hide the gold. There's no way to get away with so much weighing us down. The posse. The sheriff. Everything will be against us if we try to get out of the territory with it. So we hide it in an old mine and then come back for it next spring."

Goodale hadn't mentioned this harebrained scheme until Slocum had made it clear he wanted to discuss the matter with both McLaughlin and Glorieta. If he had ridden on back to Deadwood, he would have been dealt out entirely.

"He told me about this," Slocum said, urging her on. "He didn't say where he intended to bury the gold—only that he wanted to bury it in an old mine."

"He hasn't told me, either," Glorieta said. She dabbed at her tears but did little to dry them.

Slocum paused. She might only be repeating what she had been told to say. He couldn't tell, not through the veil of her still-flowing tears. He was getting a bad feeling about the entire robbery attempt, but he had no choice but to go along with it. For the moment.

"What's it been like up here?" he asked, suddenly changing the thrust of his questioning to catch her off guard. "I had a devil of a time finding the place."

The shift in questions didn't seem to bother Glorieta. She answered quickly. "Doug was hunting for a spot that the sheriff wouldn't find easily. We drifted around for a day or two until he hit on this place. The miner knew about it."

"Does the miner have a name?"

Glorieta shook her head. A veil of dark hair patterned a soft frame around her pale features. The tears had left streaks of grime down her face. Slocum reached over and brushed the tears still dripping down her soft cheeks.

"What about McLaughlin? Goodale thinks highly of him, but I've never run across him before."

"He seems all right. I haven't spoken much to him or Spear."

Slocum started to ask who the hell Spear was but clamped

his mouth shut. He knew Goodale well enough to know the outlaw would never try robbing the coach with only a simpleminded miner, McLaughlin, and an untried woman. Even if Slocum was able to ride along on the coach as a guard, there would still be too much danger. There had to be a few others recruited by Goodale. The difference in split would be negligible compared to the increased chances of pulling off the robbery.

Slocum smiled wryly. Goodale's cut increased significantly if he double-crossed everyone: Glorieta and McLaughlin and the miner and this Spear—and John Slocum.

"What is it, John? You look—funny."

"A thought just came to me. Goodale is no one's friend. He's certainly not mine."

"But you two—"

"We know each other. I don't owe him squat, and he doesn't owe me anything, either. There might just be a way that you and I can get a lot more from the robbery than Goodale is willing to give."

"You mean you'd cross him?" Glorieta acted as if the thought had never entered her mind. And maybe it hadn't. If she and Goodale were in cahoots, it may never have occurred to her that Slocum might be willing to double-cross Goodale, too.

"Let's just say there might be a way we can both end up richer than we'd ever dreamed of being. Are you with me on this?"

"Well, yes, surely, John. You know I love you. I'd do anything for you."

Slocum silently added, "And you'd do just about anything *to* me for that gold."

He squeezed her hand, gave her a quick kiss, and turned back to Goodale's camp. He had a long ride back to Deadwood and he had some plotting of his own to do. If anyone was going to be double-crossed, it wasn't going to be John Slocum.

12

Slocum rode slowly back to Deadwood, fragments of crosses and double-crosses turning over in his head. There was no doubt that Doug Goodale was going to try to steal Slocum's share from the robbery. What Slocum couldn't decide was Glorieta Zimmermann's involvement in the plot. She had called the outlaw leader by his first name more than once and hadn't even realized she had done so. That told Slocum she might have sold him out entirely in favor of some deal Goodale had made her.

Her sexual frontiers might extend far beyond Rod Kerwin.

But Slocum had seen the tide of greed rise in her blue eyes when he had told her he had a plan to cut Goodale out of all the gold. Half was better than the fraction Goodale would have promised. Slocum thought the woman would go along with his scheme rather than Goodale's. Avarice was a powerful tool, and he knew how to use it.

Slocum had to chuckle as he turned onto the well-traveled trail leading into Deadwood. He understood greed well because it drove him hard. Robbing the Deadwood Treasure Coach was a fool's dream. There would be guards and maybe even soldiers protecting it. Striking at the change-over point of Cold Springs was a good tactic. That might be the only vulnerable spot in Red Canyon, but it would still be very, very risky. If anyone in Goodale's gang turned tail and ran, the whole robbery would blow up in their faces.

And the risks didn't matter to Slocum because of the potential gain. Greed. He knew it all too well.

Deadwood was bustling with life as the sun went down and the saloons opened for full business. The miners came to spend their hard-won gold and the sheriff had his work cut out for him. Slocum had been gone all day, but now it was time for him to get to work.

He hated the notion of wearing the deputy's badge. He saw no reason to run in drunks, and the pay wasn't enough to step between two men ready to shoot it out. It was better to let them settle their own differences, anyway. The law had its place, Slocum reckoned, but not intruding in the day-to-day affairs of most folks.

"There you are," came the loud cry from inside the sheriff's office. The simple building holding the iron cage of the jail badly needed painting and repair. The cold September wind whistled through crevices large enough to stick a finger in. The two chairs and the sheriff's desk were in hardly better condition.

"Where the hell you been?" demanded Bullock. "I gave you the day off, not the goddamned night, too. Get your ass out there on patrol."

"Having a hard time of it, sheriff?" Slocum asked as he dismounted. The sheriff's huge frame filled the tiny door leading into the jail. "Got a full house tonight?"

"The damned cavalry's done rode into town, and it's makin' my job a living hell," Bullock said.

"Why did they come here? Is there some trouble with the Sioux?"

"There's always Indian trouble, and I wish to hell they'd get out there and tend to it. No, that fool General Adams has called 'em in to protect the stagecoach when it leaves day after tomorrow. A whole troop of those bastards. Damn them all to hell!"

Slocum had never seen Bullock this angry. He tethered his sorrel and went into the jail. The wind whipped across the sheriff's desk and scattered a pile of old wanted posters. Slocum wished he could rummage through them to see if Bullock was hunting one with the name John Slocum on it. He sat down and tried not to appear too interested in the sheriff's paperwork.

"Tell me what's happening; then I'll go on patrol."

"Get on their damned patrol is more like it," grumbled Bullock. "I sent Lowry and all the others out tonight. The troopers haven't had a leave in more'n a month. They're getting liquored up and going wild."

Slocum thought about tossing in his badge then and there. The last thing he needed was to get shot up in a drunken fight between rowdy bluecoats. Let them kill one another for all he cared. He had nothing against them personally—one by one they might be good men—but he had fought too long against the Union and seen too many of his friends and relatives cut down by Yankee bullets.

His hand touched the vest pocket where he carried his brother's watch. This was all that remained after Robert had been killed during Pickett's Charge. Pickett had been a fool, but it still had been a nameless, faceless Yankee who had killed Robert Slocum on the battlefield.

"You don't look as if you're up to it," Bullock said. "I need you now. There might even be a bonus in the job."

"What? How's that?" Slocum perked up, not at the promise of a few paltry dollars but at the offer itself. The only ways a deputy earned extra money were bribes and the occasional greenback taken off a drunk being tossed into jail.

"I been thinkin' on the stagecoach leaving with all that gold. It's a sitting duck as it travels through Red Canyon."

Slocum had to agree. Cold Springs was at the mouth of the canyon, making it the last place it was possible to hold up the treasure coach.

"I got up a few dollars from the mine owners shipping their gold over to Cheyenne," the sheriff said, "and they authorized me to pay it out if you wanted to go along as an extra guard."

"Just me?" Slocum asked, suddenly suspicious. He

remembered that Rod Kerwin had been released and sent out to spy on others thinking about robbing the coach—and the sheriff hadn't told him about it. Bullock might suspect he wasn't cut out to be a deputy.

And there was those damned wanted posters scattered on the sheriff's desk. What had Bullock found among them?

"I don't want General Adams cuttin' in on my territory," Bullock said. "The government's gettin' too big for its britches, and I resent him sayin' I can't protect the shipments leaving Deadwood."

"I can see your point," said Slocum. "How much extra are we talking?"

"Ten dollars in gold for two days' work. That's it. We ride along with the stagecoach until it's well on its way to Cheyenne."

"Where'd that be? Past Cold Springs?"

"A day past the springs, maybe to Jenny's Stockade," Bullock said. "Eleven robberies in a month." His face hardened at the thought of so much thievery in his jurisdiction. "There's not going to be an even dozen. I'll see to that."

"Catching the Bivens gang went a ways toward it," said Slocum, probing for some clue about what else the sheriff had up his sleeve. He didn't think having a small posse along with the coach was all Bullock intended.

"The Wall gang is making noises like they're going to try to rob the stagecoach," Bullock went on. "I got a line on them. We might go take them before the coach leaves."

"That's mighty ambitious," said Slocum. He scratched his chin as if considering the offer. Then he said, "I'll take the money. I can always use extra gold coins jingling in my pocket."

"Good. That makes it unanimous. Now get your butt on out and keep peace in the town. I don't want anybody gettin' themselves shot up between now 'n when the stagecoach pulls out."

Slocum checked his Colt Navy and then left, thinking hard about what Bullock had said. It sounded as if all the deputies would be accompanying the coach well past the team change at Cold Springs. This made the robbery a bit trickier—but not much, if Slocum rode with the posse.

He hadn't gone twenty paces when he heard a ruckus inside the Sunset Saloon. Heaving a sigh, Slocum went to see what the trouble might be.

Only quick reflexes saved him from being knocked over by a uniformed trooper sailing through the door. Slocum danced aside, his six-shooter in his hand before the blue-coat hit the ground. The man landed with a grunt, the air knocked from his lungs. Slocum spun, pistol trained on the man following the horse soldier from the saloon.

"Don't even think about it," Slocum said in a low voice that cut through the din from inside like a knife slicing through lard. The man growled and turned, ready for a fight. He stopped dead in his tracks when he saw the six-gun in Slocum's steady hand.

"You wouldn't kill me. Not for roughin' up scum like him. I can tell by your accent you're a Johnny Reb, too."

"Right now I'm supposed to keep things quiet in Dead-wood," Slocum said. "There's a couple ways of doing that. The first is for you to get on back to your drinking and forget the horse soldier. The other is for me to blow out your heart. Nothing's as peaceful as a corpse. What's it to be?"

The miner growled deep in his throat, balled his fists so tight they looked like quart jars with knuckles, then advanced on Slocum. A single shot would only enrage the drunk miner. Slocum sidestepped the first awkward punch. If it had landed, he would have been dead. The miner worked all day in a mine, carting ore and swinging a pick. Slocum knew better than to let him get a second chance.

Slocum stepped up and swung his Colt as hard as he could. The sound of metal breaking bone sounded louder than a gunshot. The miner clutched the side of his head, then sank to the boardwalk, unconscious.

Two of the miner's friends stood in the saloon's doorway. Slocum faced them, six-shooter still in his hand. "Why don't you get your friend on over to the doc's office? He needs patching up more than he needs another drink."

The men weren't as liquored up as their friend and were less inclined to take on a deputy with a drawn pistol. They kept a wary eye on Slocum, but they obeyed, heaving the miner to his feet and dragging him across the street toward the only doctor in town. Slocum wondered if they would find Dr. Magee in or not. The man was more than likely out having himself a royal toot.

Slocum watched the trio until they reached the far side of the broad main street, then went to see what condition the horse soldier was in. The man moaned weakly and struck out when Slocum poked him with the toe of his boot.

"Wh—"

"Get up and move along," Slocum said. "You just got thrown out of the saloon."

"Can't do that. Won't let them," the man muttered. Slocum shoved him back to the street and held him down with his foot. In the light, he saw the man was a sergeant.

"Don't press your luck. You want another drink?" Slocum asked, hit with a bolt of inspiration. "I'll buy it if you promise to stay out of trouble the rest of the night— and keep any of your company out of trouble, too."

"You'd buy me a drink?" The sergeant stared up at Slocum with bleary eyes. "Nobody in this whole damn town's been civil to us. Who the hell are you?"

"The law," Slocum said. The words tasted bitter on his tongue. He couldn't wait for the next forty-eight hours to pass so he could throw away the badge on his vest and be done with this playacting.

"You're the sheriff?"

"A deputy just wanting to keep the peace. Here." Slocum offered his left hand to help the horse soldier up. The sergeant accepted it and got to shaky feet. He held his battered head and then sucked in a deep, steadying breath.

"I'm worse off than I thought. Never had to let a lawman do that for me."

"Do you want the drink or not?"

"I do, sir. I surely do."

Slocum slid his Colt back into the soft leather cross-draw holster and walked to one side of the sergeant. As they made their way up the main street of Deadwood, the soldier's steps grew stronger and more confident. By the time they reached the Last Frontier Saloon, he was sober again.

"Hit my head when I went down back there," the sergeant said. "On the bar. Worst of it was, I spilt my drink." He brushed at the front of his uniform. It was so stained and dirty Slocum couldn't tell if whiskey added to the untidiness or not.

Slocum studied the room before moving to a corner where he could sit with his back to the wall and keep an eye out. Bullock hadn't told him how to keep the peace. If he could win over the horse soldier, this might help head off other violence. It was apparent the townspeople didn't cotton much to the arrogant cavalry troopers.

"You under the command of General Adams?" asked Slocum as he poured a drink from the bottle he had ordered.

"That I am. The general's a fine soldier, one of the best. He's been entrusted with seeing that the mail gets through untouched by the brigands in the area."

"No easy job," Slocum said. "It gets even harder when there's an army payroll on the same stagecoach."

"How'd you know that?"

"I'm a deputy. The general told the sheriff. How long you boys going to be in the Deadwood area?"

"We're leaving day after tomorrow. Escort for the coach."

Slocum snorted and shook his head.

"What's the matter?" demanded the sergeant. "Don't you think we can protect the mail shipment?"

"It's not that," Slocum said. "There's just other ways of doing it without riding along and acting like a sitting duck."

"What are you talking about?" The sergeant knocked back a quick drink and took another, as if daring Slocum to stop him. This was the last thing on Slocum's mind.

"You're fighting a defensive war. That's no good. There's hardly ever been a sound defensive battle won. Remember the Alamo? The Mexicans trapped them inside.

They didn't stand a chance. The only way to win is to take the offensive."

"How can we do that?" The sergeant looked confused. Slocum poured him another drink.

"Don't wait for the road agents to come to you. Go after them. There're a half dozen bands of men out there in the Black Hills living off the sweat of the miners. Not more than two or three of the highwaymen are able to even think of robbing the Deadwood Treasure Coach."

"Only two or three?"

"Sure. The Bill Bivens gang. Tough hombres. Then there's Wall and his gang. Worst of the bunch is the Doug Goodale gang. Stop them and you can prevent *any* mail coach robbery."

"Why's that?"

"The rest of the road agents working the Cut-Off Trail aren't stupid. If they see the worst of them can't pull off the robbery, they'll crawl back into their holes. For a while, at least."

"Bivens, Wall, and Goodale?"

"Those are the three most notorious." Slocum felt a warmth rising inside. He had planted the seeds of the double-cross in this sergeant. The noncom would do some asking around and find that Bullock had already jailed most of the Bivens gang. It wouldn't be much longer, Slocum reckoned, before the Wall gang was shot up and on the run. That was what Sheriff Bullock had intimated earlier.

That left only the notorious Doug Goodale gang for the cavalry to go after. By the time the gold-laden coach left Deadwood, the horse soldiers would be hunting down Goodale's camp.

Slocum would show the treacherous Doug Goodale what a double-cross was really like.

13

Dog tired, Slocum dragged himself back to the ramshackle jailhouse. He could barely keep his eyes open. It had been a hell of a night for keeping the peace in Deadwood. Although he could have teamed up with another of the deputies making the rounds, he had steered clear of them. He still didn't like the glint in Lowry's eye whenever he looked in Slocum's direction. If he couldn't find anything wrong, Lowry was the kind to make it up. The only consolation Slocum could find in the deputy's animosity toward him was that he hadn't made any outrageous accusations to arouse the sheriff's suspicions.

If he had found a wanted poster, he would have shot Slocum in the back and collected the reward. As it stood, Slocum thought the deputy only suspected.

"It's about time you got back," Seth Bullock said in his booming voice. The man's entire chest rumbled when he spoke. This time the words carried like cannonade. "We got work to do. Serious work, too." He spun the cylinder in his ivory-handled six-shooter.

"I've been in most of the saloons along Main Street," Slocum said. "The ones over on Pine aren't too busy tonight, all things considered. If you want me to—"

"I want you to get your ass in here."

Slocum slipped into the jailhouse and saw that the other deputies were crowded together in one corner of the small office. Lowry glared at him but made no move for his pistol. Slocum took that to mean he still hadn't been found out. He heaved a sigh of relief that he only had another day of this charade before he could toss the star onto the ground and ride off.

With any luck, he'd be riding on with enough gold to keep him happy for a long, long time.

"We're going after the Wall gang," Bullock said.

Slocum closed his eyes for a moment and tried not to groan. He had been walking from one end of Deadwood to the other and back all night. He wasn't inclined to go riding into the sunrise to find a notorious band of road agents.

"I've got word that they're hidin' just outside of town, waitin' for the stagecoach to leave tomorrow." Bullock craned his neck around and peered out the door at the rising sun. "We don't have much time. If we wait any longer, they might have hightailed it and we'll never find 'em."

Slocum filed out with the others. He had planted the seeds in the cavalry sergeant's head that there were only three gangs to worry about. He would find out in short order that Bullock had already broken the back of the Bivens gang. Slocum couldn't carp too much if Bullock wanted to add the Wall gang to that roster. This made it all the more likely that General Adams could be nudged into going after Doug Goodale. The officer wasn't going to take kindly to having the Deadwood sheriff round up *all* the outlaws in Dakota Territory.

"I heard tell Wall is holed up over near the Whitewood cemetery," Bullock said when he got his men assembled outside. "Lowry, you and Slocum go on through town, cut across the creek, and come in from the far side. I'll spread the others out to catch those rats when you flush them and they try to run."

"How long before you'll be in position, sheriff?" asked Lowry.

"Before you get there," Bullock snapped. "That's why you're goin' the long way around." The sheriff looked at Slocum. "Don't you two get into any trouble, hear?"

"I won't start anything," Slocum said. He wondered if he could just gun Lowry down when they were out of sight of the others. From the wildfire burning in the deputy, he doubted it. The man would never give him the chance. If anything, it was Slocum who had to watch his back. Lowry was all fired up and ready to kill anything that moved as he had done before during the Bivens gang's capture.

"Don't," the sheriff warned. He motioned to the others to get their horses. Lowry and Slocum mounted and started off. The deputy set a quick trot as the pace. Slocum trailed behind, not wanting to rush matters. He knew Bullock had given him and Lowry the most dangerous position. They had to frighten the Wall gang into running into the sheriff's open arms.

If they didn't panic, if they stood and fought, there'd only be two guns against more than a dozen.

"Speed it up," Lowry called. "Unless you're turning chicken. Is that it? You got a yellow streak running up your spine?"

"Not so's you'd ever know it," Slocum said. "I don't think it's a good idea to wear out the horses this early. We might need some speed later on."

"To run?" sneered Lowry.

"To go chasing down any of the gang who decides to make a break for it," Slocum corrected.

Lowry grumbled and said something under his breath that Slocum missed. He didn't much care what the rangy deputy said or did as long as it didn't affect him. They rode in silence for fifteen minutes, got to the creek, and cut due west. The cold water splashing up from his sorrel's hooves brought Slocum to full wakefulness.

"There," said Lowry. "There's a campfire. We got the bastards! Let's go!"

"Hold on," Slocum cautioned. "Let's be sure the sheriff is in position—and let's take a few minutes to scout out their camp."

"Coward."

"Just using my head, which is something you aren't doing. Is there a sentry posted? If the guard sees us, we'll be drawing flies before noon."

"Chickenshit," snarled Lowry. The deputy was past caring about his personal safety. He drew his Winchester from a saddle scabbard, levered a round into the chamber, and reared back in the saddle. His horse bucked, then Lowry started for the outlaw camp at a dead gallop.

Slocum had half a mind to let the fool go in alone. If he did, though, it would go against him when Bullock found out. Slocum considered the chances of the sheriff ever learning that Slocum had let Lowry lead the way to dying. Someone would mention it. One of the road agents, another deputy who had sneaked in close enough to watch, someone. Slocum had to keep up the pretense of being a lawman for just one more day. Tomorrow he would ride out with Bullock and the others to protect the Deadwood Treasure Coach. After the stagecoach arrived at Cold Springs and Goodale got the gold, Slocum could stop being a hypocrite. It was hell what he had to do to steal a few hundred pounds of gold.

The first bullet from Lowry's rifle shattered the stillness of the morning. The deputy let out a rebel yell and raced forward, rifle firing wildly. Slocum followed at a distance, ready to turn back any of the outlaws getting past the rampaging deputy.

He saw Lowry shoot down three men still in their bedrolls. The surprise attack was going about as Slocum had thought it would. The deputy wasn't even giving the gang a chance to surrender. If he could get them in his sights, he'd cut them down.

"Give it up!" Slocum bellowed over the gunfire. "We've got you surrounded. Don't try to run!"

A bullet took his hat off. Slocum ducked low and aimed the best he could from horseback. His bullet caught a man in the belly, doubling him over. The outlaw kicked and tried to bring himself back to a sitting position. He was in too much pain to do so. Slocum got off three more shots that caused a fluttering of hands to rise in the pale morning sun.

"That's it, mister. Don't kill us!" cried one outlaw. "We give up!"

Lowry was still on a tear, riding back and forth through the Wall gang's camp. He drew a bead on one man whose hands were high in the air. Something caused the deputy to pause and look around.

He stared straight down the barrel of Slocum's Colt Navy.

"Go on, Lowry," Slocum said. "Pull the trigger."

"You wouldn't kill me. This one's scum. The son of a bitch is a criminal. He doesn't deserve anything but being cut down."

"He's already given himself up. I don't let anybody kill my prisoners."

"You—" Lowry's curse was cut off by Bullock's arrival. The sheriff and the other four deputies came crashing into the camp from the south. Slocum wasn't sure what startled the sheriff more. Seeing the entire gang docile and ready to be led off was a shock. But seeing one of his deputies ready to blow the head off another was a tad worse.

"What the hell's going on?" demanded Bullock.

"Got 'em ready for you, sheriff," said Slocum. "I just wanted to keep them alive." His aim on Lowry's head didn't waver.

"Put that down, dammit," said Bullock. "They're the ones we shoot, not each other."

"We don't kill men who have given themselves up," Slocum said. The loathing he felt for Lowry was compounded by all the senseless murder he had seen during the war. More than once a Yankee company had run over the Confederate line, killing anyone who moved. It didn't matter if they tried to surrender; they got cut down. It was easier to slaughter than to deal with wounded prisoners.

The South might have been equally guilty when it came to taking prisoners, but his unit had always tried to do right; as a captain, Slocum saw to that then and he was seeing to it now.

Slocum eased back on the hammer, letting it down slowly. He wanted to kill Lowry. He should have gone ahead and done it when he had the chance. The kill-crazy look in the man's eyes was now directed solely at Slocum. It wouldn't matter if he found a wanted poster. He would gun down Slocum the first chance he got.

"Get 'em in a circle. Good. Go on, hog-tie 'em and start 'em back to town. All but that one." Bullock pointed to a paunchy man at the edge of the camp. He had been moving a half step at a time toward a stand of trees with an eye toward running for his freedom. The sheriff's singling him out put an end to any such attempt.

"Come on over here, Danny boy," said Bullock. "Gentlemen, this here's the leader of the Wall gang."

"Go to hell, Bullock," snarled the captured outlaw. "We ain't done nothin'. You can't arrest us for just campin' here all peaceful-like."

"I'm arresting you for plotting to rob the stagecoach tomorrow. I got word you've been workin' on it for well nigh a month now."

"A man can talk. I wasn't going to do anything. I was just shootin' off my mouth."

Bullock dismounted and motioned for Lowry and Slocum to do likewise. "Go through this yahoo's bedroll and see if you can find any plans for the robbery. That's evidence enough that he's a stinking liar."

Lowry found a packet of papers wrapped in oilskin. He tore the cloth back and pulled out a thick sheaf of papers. The deputy blankly stared at them for an instant, then passed them over to Bullock. Slocum saw then that Lowry couldn't read.

He didn't know if this was a relief or not. Lowry wouldn't have been able to find a wanted poster on him, but that didn't mean the smeary, indistinct picture that usually accompanied the flyers wouldn't have alerted him to Slocum's past deeds.

"Yep, this here's what I been hearin' about," said Bullock. "See?" He held up one map of the Cut-Off Trail showing four spots marked with large X's. "These are places where there's been a robbery in the past month or so. If I read this right, you're responsible for no fewer than a quarter of all the robberies occurrin' in Red Canyon. What do you have to say about that, Wall?"

"Prove it." The outlaw's voice almost broke, though, showing he was starting to have second thoughts about getting off scot-free.

"Yes sir, this is a right good detailed plan for robbing the coach tomorrow. You were plannin' on takin' the stagecoach near Cold Springs, weren't you, Wall?"

The highwayman clamped his mouth shut and didn't say a word. Slocum moved around a bit to get a better look at Lowry. He wanted to be sure the deputy didn't simply gun down his prisoner rather than letting him live to stand trial.

The move put Lowry on his guard. He glanced uneasily between their prisoner and Slocum, trying to decide what to do. He finally took his finger off the trigger of his rifle and glared hard at Slocum.

"A complete plan, and it was in your possession. How many of your men do you think will be willing to spill their guts in exchange for convicting you, Wall? One, two? All of them?"

"They're all liars. You can't believe a word any of them say," said Wall.

Bullock laughed. "Get him back to jail. We just done a real good day's work. The stagecoach can leave tomorrow and not worry about being robbed now that Wall and Bivens are both in my jailhouse. Yes, sir, a good day's work."

Slocum smiled grimly. The competition was eliminated. Now all he had to do was work a bit more to be sure that Doug Goodale couldn't pull off his double-cross. Then Slocum would be as rich as any railroad magnate. Richer!

14

"Good work, men," Seth Bullock said as he tossed the cell keys onto his desk. He drew his ivory-handled pistol and laid it beside the key ring to show that the morning's work was done. "We wiped out them vipers good and the stage is going to be as safe as if it was in my hip pocket when it leaves tomorrow."

"There might be others," complained Lowry. "We don't know that Wall and Bivens were the only road agents planning to rob the coach. Those thieves grow like mushrooms in shit."

"There'll be protection aplenty when the stagecoach leaves," Bullock said. He turned and spat authoritatively to emphasize his words. He hit the battered cuspidor dead center. "Get the town in order today, and we can take a couple days off to escort the coach beyond Cold Springs. After that, it's up to the stage line to protect their own damned gold and passengers."

"I heard tell there's going to be a military payroll aboard," chimed in another deputy. "Why not let them horse soldiers do the guardin' and give us some time off? My feet are killing me from walking all night."

"He's got a point, sheriff," said Slocum, wanting to add fuel to the fire. "We can't do a danged thing that General

Adams and his men couldn't do. Why not give us the day off?"

"Dammit," flared the sheriff. "I'm responsible for this town. It's got a bad reputation, and it isn't deserved. Just because Hickok upped and got himself shot in the back like he did, everyone thinks poorly of Deadwood. This is going to be a law-abiding town if I have to hang every man jack in it!"

"There's always Captain Crawford over in Custer City," said Slocum, still agitating. "I'm sure he'd lend you a few of his vigilantes if you asked real nice."

"We take care of our own. *I* take care of the law in Deadwood, not some scatterbrained bunch of vigilantes who don't know their asses from the end of their guns."

Slocum fell silent. He had done as much as he could to rile the sheriff without being obvious. He silently thanked the other deputy for giving him the opportunity. But Slocum also wished the sheriff would ease up just a mite. The other deputy's feet weren't the only ones aching from too much walking. Slocum was about as tired as he could remember, and tomorrow was going to require his full attention.

The robbery had to go well, and then the double-cross had to work even better, if he was to get the entire treasure trove being shipped on the stagecoach.

"You're right about needing some rest. Go on, catch some shut-eye," Bullock said, "but be back here for the dusk patrol. I don't want *any* trouble in Deadwood tonight, and I sure as hell don't want any of you screwing up tomorrow. That stagecoach is going to get through."

Slocum left the jail quickly, wanting to avoid Lowry. He got only a few steps before he heard the clicking of the deputy's boot heels behind him. He slipped the leather thong off his Colt's hammer and readied himself to draw.

"Slocum!"

He turned, his hand in motion. Slocum stopped the draw when he saw that Lowry just stood in the street, hands at his sides.

"What do you want?"

"It's not over between us. I want a piece of you, and I'm

going to get it. You're a lily-livered, no-account, good-for-nothing son of a bitch!"

Slocum didn't respond. The other man wanted him to draw first. Slocum just stared and let Lowry do all the talking.

"Didn't you hear me? Are you deaf as well as stupid?"

Slocum's cold green eyes bored holes in Lowry. The other man's abuse tapered off and finally died out altogether. He was ready to draw on Slocum but Slocum never gave him the chance.

"I want to go rest. Putting up with you has been real exhausting," said Slocum. He turned, every sense straining. He listened for the whisper of metal against leather. He listened for Lowry's sharp intake of breath that would signal the man going for his six-shooter. Slocum even sniffed hard at the wind trying to get Lowry's spoor. Fear rode the gentle breeze blowing toward him, and it was all Lowry's scent. The man was at the breaking point. He either had to back down or try to shoot Slocum from behind.

Lowry backed down.

"This ain't the end of it," he cried. "We'll have it out, you damned coward!"

For his part, Slocum would have gladly gunned the deputy down. He had the provocation and knew several curious onlookers would have backed him up. But he was too near being able to chuck the badge and get on with thieving. He didn't want to do anything that would jinx the stagecoach robbery.

He went directly to the saloon that most of the bluecoats had staked out as their own. He pushed inside the swinging doors and looked around. First one, then another of the horse soldiers saw him. The general din died down as he walked in.

"Howdy, mister," came the sergeant's cheerful greeting. "What brings you in here? Can I buy you a drink?"

"Reckon you might," Slocum said. At the sergeant's words, the others turned back to their drinking. Everything must be all right if their sergeant greeted this civilian lawman.

"What's been going on?" the sergeant asked. "This don't look like a social visit. None of my boys are in trouble, are they?"

"Nothing like that," Slocum said. "Just wanted to tell you that the sheriff rounded up the entire Wall gang this morning, just a bit after sunrise. Got the lot of them—and they were planning on taking the coach tomorrow."

"He got *all* of 'em?"

"That he did," said Slocum, sipping at the sergeant's whiskey.

"Damn. The general's going to be madder 'n a wet hen over this. He was sent out here to make sure the mail got through. *Him*, not some tin star local sheriff."

"There's always the Goodale gang. Heard tell they're planning to make an attempt on the coach," said Slocum.

"The Goodale gang? Never heard of 'em."

"They're bad ones. Hell and damnation, Sheriff Bullock can't even find them. Clever bastards."

The sergeant got a shrewd look in his eye as he poured Slocum another drink. "Tell me, deputy, how's your sheriff intendin' to round up these desperadoes?"

"Can't do it," Slocum admitted, sipping some more of the whiskey. "That's why he's having the entire mess of us deputies ride shotgun on the stage. He figures if he can't find Goodale, then Goodale will find us sooner or later. Risky. I told him it's risky, but—" Slocum shook his head as if he had tried and failed to convince the sheriff of the danger to the gold shipment.

"Then Bullock's not got any plans for trackin' down this Goodale?"

"Like I said, Goodale's too clever for him. Good drinking your whiskey, sergeant. Thank you." Slocum rose and tipped his hat in the noncom's direction. He heard the sergeant bellowing orders before he got out of the saloon. In ten minutes, the sergeant's superior would hear all about the treacherous Doug Goodale gang. In twenty, the lieutenant would be reporting directly to General Adams.

Things were going along just fine in Deadwood. It was time to give them a little push in Goodale's camp. Slocum rode out of town, humming a happy tune.

The steep walls of the canyon rose around him, threatening to crush together. Slocum threw off the notion he might be nothing more than a bug caught in a vise. He was playing a dangerous lone hand and he knew it. There wasn't a speck of doubt in his mind that Doug Goodale meant to double-cross him—or at least try. And Slocum was as sure as he could be that Glorieta was in cahoots with the outlaw.

He thought a bit on the woman as he rode. She was about the prettiest thing he had come across in months and months. It was too bad about her husband and family. Slocum attributed the way her mind twisted and turned like a sidewinder to the deaths. She might have been a faithful wife and as honest as the day was long before. Not now. Glorieta Zimmermann was like a wild colt, free and running without control. Slocum wondered if his promise to cut her in if she'd help him double-cross Goodale was enough to make her switch allegiances.

He hoped so. He would hate to have to kill her if she threw in with Goodale.

Slocum spotted the miner on sentry duty. As before, the man was worthless. Whatever he did, he paid no attention to the trail and anyone on it. Slocum considered sneaking into camp, then dismissed the notion. He didn't want Goodale to get too suspicious.

He kept riding on past the sentry and into the outlaw camp. The only one he saw was McLaughlin. The man looked up and frowned as if he expected someone other than Slocum.

Slocum dismounted and tethered his horse. "Where's Goodale?" he asked. "I got some important news for him."

McLaughlin shrugged. "He was around here somewhere earlier. Don't rightly know where he got off to."

Slocum poured himself a cup of bitter coffee and sipped at it, looking over the bent rim at McLaughlin. The man stirred uneasily. Slocum wished he could play poker with him. It would be like stealing from a baby. McLaughlin had no control over the apprehension flooding his features. He stood suddenly, rubbed sweaty hands on his canvas pants, and said, "I think he might be upslope a ways. I'll go see if I can get him down here."

"Much obliged," Slocum said. He watched McLaughlin hurry off. He almost laughed. The man was supposed to be arranging for extra horses. Although they wouldn't be needed to tote the gold, they would come in handy in outrunning any pursuit. A man with two horses could run a posse into the ground and be in Canada before they caught their breaths.

Slocum perked up when he thought he heard the sound of a horse. Before he could even turn in that direction, he heard approaching steps.

"Slocum!" came Doug Goodale's cheerful call. "Didn't expect to see you. Is everything all right back in Deadwood?"

"Can't say. Set a spell and let's go over everything. This might be a problem or it might not be."

Goodale looked at him, his eyes cagey. "There can't be any problem I haven't thought of. The plan's perfection— unless we can't hit them at Cold Springs."

"That's still the best place," Slocum said. "But I just found out General Adams is leading a cavalry company. They'll be out for blood if anyone tries to take the payroll and the mail pouch."

"Hell, John," he said easily, "they'd have blood in their eye if anybody stole the gold. What's a few extra horse soldiers going to mean to us?"

"Could mean a great deal if they're accompanying the stagecoach. I'll be riding with the sheriff and can decoy him away, but there's no way I'll be able to do that with the troopers. This Adams isn't easy to deal with, from all that's being said about him."

"Well—" Goodale said, picking up a green stick and poking idly at the campfire as he thought. A few embers spilled from the tiny fire pit. He kicked them back with the toe of his boot; then he came to a decision. "We'll take the chance. We've got to go through with this, John. It's too good to pass up. Do you have any suggestions as to how to get around this Adams?"

"I might be able to send him on a wild-goose chase," Slocum said, measuring his response to match Goodale's. He didn't want to seem too eager. "Can you give me somewhere I might be able to send him?"

"You want me to fake a camp and lay a false trail?" Goodale tossed the stick into the fire and rubbed his chin. "That's a real fine idea, John. I knew I was doin' the right thing throwing in with you."

"Tell me where. Better yet, make a map, then tear off part of it. The military loves solving tactical problems."

"I'll do that very thing." Goodale rummaged in his bedroll and came out with a tattered piece of paper. He frowned as he concentrated on drawing passes and mountains with the stub of a pencil. He rubbed part of it off, then passed it to Slocum. "That's specific enough to get the general's attention, but not so good that he'll be able to find the campsite soon."

"You'll send McLaughlin over to lay the trail?"

"Hell, this is lookin' to be so much fun, I might do it myself," answered Goodale.

"Then everything is ready for tomorrow," Slocum said.

"Reckon so. Wish me luck, John. This is going to make us all rich."

Slocum shook Goodale's hand, then said, "Aren't you forgetting something?"

"What?" The outlaw looked startled. The mask descended quickly and covered his reaction. "Can't think of anything—"

"Where are we going to meet up after the robbery? I'll need to know where the gold is so I can get back here come spring."

"Oh, that. Sorry, it slipped my mind. Got so much going on," Goodale apologized. "All right. Here's Cold Springs. We'll take the gold and make for these hills. I've scouted out a mine shaft that is just about everything we could want. It's right here. The name's the Winsome Lass. Big sign out on the road 'bout here. Head straight up the hill and wind around a mite and you'll see the mouth of the mine. Can't miss it. We'll be draggin' the gold in by the time you get there, I reckon."

Slocum made a pretense of studying the map, then erased it with his boot. "I've got it." He stood, then paused as if remembering something. "I want to say good-bye to Glorieta. Is she around camp?"

"Last I saw of her, she was up there. She's mighty down in the mouth about not being allowed to come with us. Never saw a filly so eager to hold up a stagecoach. You might cheer her up."

"What's to become of her?" asked Slocum, still playing Goodale's game.

"I told her we would meet up with her over in Boise. She's leaving in the morning, going to Jenny's Stockade and then on over to the railroad. I gave her enough money for the ticket."

"That's probably best, getting her out of the way like this," Slocum said. "I won't be long."

"Take your time, John. I've got to get this fake camp set up so it'll convince a hot-for-blood army general."

Goodale laughed as he spun and jumped onto his horse. The animal shied. Goodale got it under control and then put his heels to its flanks, racing off in the direction of the bogus camp. Slocum watched until Goodale was gone from sight. He didn't doubt the outlaw would do a good job. Getting General Adams off his trail was worth a considerable amount of planning and effort.

Slocum turned uphill and found Glorieta sitting and staring into space. She jumped when he touched her shoulder.

"John!" She turned away, looking down the long, winding road through Red Canyon. "You surprised me. I didn't hear you come up."

"Is everything all right?" he asked. She didn't answer right away. "Goodale's gone for a while. He's getting a decoy ready for us to lure General Adams away from the chase tomorrow."

"This is going to work, isn't it?" she asked. He read the worry in her voice.

"It will unless you get cold feet," he said.

"I—I love you, John. I wouldn't betray you."

"I didn't say that. You have to be like a melodeon player and act out your role. Goodale can't suspect a thing. If he catches even a whiff of double-cross, he'll kill you."

"I know. He's so smiling and kind most of the time, but then he turns nasty. It's as if he's two men put into one man's body. I don't understand him."

Slocum wondered what had gone on between Glorieta and Goodale. He didn't ask.

"Has he said anything more about his plans after the robbery? Where he's going to stash the gold?"

"No, but he can't get too far from Cold Springs with it. He's planning on at least five hundred pounds, or so he told me."

Slocum nodded. He could believe the take would be that much. But he expected Goodale to leave some small hint to tantalize him.

"He did say he was thinking about putting it in some mine shaft—the Winsome Lad."

"Winsome Lass," Slocum corrected. He was happier now. The stories all meshed. He didn't doubt that Goodale was planning on double-crossing Glorieta, too. It only made sense.

"Oh, John, I don't know what I've got myself into. I don't want to be a part of the robbery. All I know is shopkeeping and being a wife. This is too confusing for me."

"You're doing just fine," he said. "Are you with me in this? If not, you can just ride on out and never look back. It's not too late to quit."

"No, I promised you. You—you're playing straight. And after all you've done for me, I couldn't walk away from you. I just couldn't!"

He held her tightly, letting her bury her face in his shoulder. He felt hot tears soaking into his shirt. She looked up, her blue eyes welling with more tears.

"I need you, John. I need you to tell me it's going to be all right, that this is going to work out for the best."

"It will. Just don't be in camp tomorrow. When Goodale

and the others leave, you get the hell out, too. Trail them, be sure you know where he is going to hide the gold. And then don't come back here."

"Why not? Doug wanted to finish the robbery, hide the gold, then come back through here to pick up the spare horses."

"I'm sending General Adams here. It's the only way I can be sure the army isn't going to put in an appearance during the robbery. The general will have Indian scouts with him that will know instantly if a camp's been used for long. Goodale isn't going to be able to fake one well enough to fool an Indian."

"This is so complicated!" she moaned.

He kissed her to stop her from complaining further. He was taking a chance trusting her this far. Slocum still didn't know if he wanted to share the gold with her. The kiss deepened and he decided that he did. He was offering her far more than Goodale ever could. And he was offering her an equal split, something the outlaw would never have done.

Glorieta's tongue stroked eagerly across the tip of his, then boldly pushed into his mouth. Her arms tightened around him as she pulled him closer. He felt the softness of her breasts crushing down between them. She pulled back, breathless.

"I want you now, John. I want you!"

"We can't—" He looked around. There wasn't any good place to lie down. The rocky slopes provided no trace of softness with only the sparsest vegetation. What little grew up here was prickly and uninviting.

"Now," she insisted. Her hand stroked over his crotch. The lump growing there convinced him that he wanted her as badly as she did him.

They stood. Slocum dropped his gun belt and began unbuttoning his trousers. She pushed his hands away and began doing it for him. Her hot breath gusted through the ever-widening opening and aroused him even more. When he sprang out, her impatient mouth engulfed his length.

Slocum gasped and almost lost his balance. Glorieta sucked hard on him, trying to pull his innards out through the end of his fleshy stalk. He laced his fingers through her dark hair and guided her in a slower, more deliberate rhythm. He wanted this delightful mouthing to go on forever. The way she worked her lips and tongue across his excited flesh made him worry he was going to explode at any minute like a stick of dynamite with a lit fuse.

"I want more than this, John," she said, pulling free of his shaft. "I want to feel you inside me."

"But how?"

She stood and hiked her skirt. Her hand gripped him firmly and pulled him up under her skirt. He felt the wet gash and knew that anything was possible now. Glorieta hopped clumsily until Slocum put his arm around her waist and steadied her. She stood on tiptoe on her left foot and locked her right leg around his waist. Wiggling back and forth settled him firmly inside her.

"This is paradise," she cooed. "I want more. I want to feel you trying to rip me apart!"

Slocum began lifting and dropping her, just a little at first and then with increasing confidence in his motion. He almost left her clinging nether lips, then let gravity pull her back. With her her leg wrapped around him, there wasn't any chance they would lose contact. Slocum just worried that he might lose his balance and they would both go tumbling downhill. If they did, they'd do it together, in the most delightful way possible.

His breathing became harsher, deeper, as his arousal mounted. His loins burned with the motion of the woman's body against his. He cupped her buttocks and squeezed down hard. Glorieta gasped in response to this carnal handling.

"I love the way you feel, John," she gasped out. She twisted from side to side and finally couldn't stand the mounting tensions inside her any longer. She kicked with her left foot and wrapped both her legs around Slocum's strong body.

He sank balls deep into the woman's clinging interior. Her inner muscles twitched and worked at his shaft, milking him. He felt the hot tide rising within, but couldn't stop it.

Just as he gasped out, Glorieta clung fiercely to him. Her nails cut through his shirt and raked at his back. Her hips went wild and then subsided.

"So nice," she murmured. Her long legs released their death grip on his waist and she sank to the ground.

The woman looked up at him and Slocum couldn't read her expression. He had just made love to her and he didn't know if she would try to betray him to Doug Goodale.

It didn't matter. He was going to make sure *he* was the one doing the double-crossing.

15

Slocum rode out of Goodale's camp the next morning feeling like the cat that had devoured the canary. He smiled and tried not to wipe the feathers from his face. Things had gone better than he had hoped. Goodale was going to double-cross him; he was sure of that. And it didn't much matter what Glorieta did. If she told Goodale that Slocum was sending the cavalry into the camp after the robbery, it just meant another problem for Goodale. He wouldn't be able to take enough horses with him for the robbery.

No matter what happened, Goodale had to stash the gold somewhere and then hightail it. Slocum intended to find out where the gold was and get to it right away. If necessary, he could have it out with Goodale, but Slocum didn't think it would come to that.

For all his talk, the outlaw wasn't going to put the gold in any mine shaft and blow the tunnel to seal in the loot. Slocum couldn't see Doug Goodale working as a miner to get even a quarter ton of gold out in the springtime. He reckoned Goodale was going to stash the gold, but not under a mountain of rock. He would dump it, maybe in an old mine, and then come back for it in a few weeks when the ruckus was over and the robbery had then cooled down a mite. To blast a mine now was about the same as putting up a sign showing where the gold was to any posse on his trail.

Goodale was smarter than that—and Slocum was even smarter.

Slocum rode back into Deadwood, his mind turning over all the things he needed to do. He had a passel to do and only a little time to finish everything. The Deadwood Treasure Coach was going to be pulling out somewhere around noon, if the rumors were right. From his cautious checking and the little details Bullock had let slip, he guessed that was about right.

The town buzzed with anticipation. Slocum didn't have to listen to the conversations among the citizens to know what the big topic was. Sitting at the end of the main street, looking fit for any European king to ride in, was the stagecoach. The huge Concord had been specially outfitted with iron sheeting for this trip. Slocum didn't have to ask to know there weren't going to be many paying customers going through to Cheyenne. The only people inside would be guards hired by the Gilmer, Saulsbury, and Patrick Stage Company and a few staunch souls who were sure that nothing could ever go wrong.

He dismounted and led his horse to the stable. The tow-headed boy perked up when he saw Slocum enter.

"Hi, deputy," the boy called. "I done everything you said. I got the horses waiting. You think it's gonna be all right to just leave 'em out on the road like that?"

Slocum chuckled and said, "It will be fine. Nobody's going to come along and steal the sheriff's spare horses. How many did you put in the remuda?"

"I rounded up the strongest ones I could find, just like you asked. There's only six, though."

"So?" asked Slocum.

"But I seen the posse forming. There's nine in it. Ten if you're added in, too." The boy smiled proudly. "I been workin' on my addin' and subtractin' and I can cipher with the best."

"I'm sure you can." Slocum worked over the problems in his mind. The boy had no idea he was helping with robbing the stagecoach. When Goodale hid the gold, Slocum would swoop down and move it. With any luck, he might even be able to leave the gold loaded on the horses the stableboy had staked out for him. He didn't like fooling the boy the way he had, and the sheriff was going to be madder than a wet hen when he got the bill for the horses from the stable's owner. Slocum had seen no reason to pay for the horses himself. As long as the stable hand thought they were for the sheriff, he'd keep his mouth shut.

By the time Seth Bullock straightened the mess out, Slocum intended to be long gone from Dakota Territory.

"Want me to curry your horse, deputy?" The boy's eyes glowed. He thought he was helping out.

"Going to be leaving soon. The sorrel's in good shape. Give her some oats and a bit of water, but not too much. Don't want her bloating when I hit the trail."

Slocum started to leave, then paused as if remembering something important. He motioned for the boy to come over. The boy's blond head bobbed up and down when Slocum asked, "Can you do something real important for me?"

"Sure, deputy. Anything!"

"I've got to get a message to General Adams."

"The general!"

"None other," Slocum said. "I came across what might be the Goodale gang's camp. If you go over and tell the sergeant what I'm going to tell you, there'll be a nice reward in it for you."

"But you scouted out the camp."

"I just saw the camp. Didn't see anyone in it. Besides, I got to ride with the sheriff. This is the cavalry's business." Slocum didn't know how this lie would be received. The boy took it all in and bobbed his head even faster, making Slocum think of a chicken pecking at corn in a barnyard.

"I'll do it, sir. Anything you want."

"It's only fair for you to get the reward," Slocum went on. "As a lawman, I'm not entitled to it, and I doubt if the stable owner's paying you all that much."

"I can't complain," the boy said in a tone that meant

it wouldn't do him any good to gripe. The promise of the reward from General Adams went a long way toward insuring the boy's cooperation.

"Here's the layout of their camp." Slocum sketched it in the dust. "You memorize it or even draw it on paper to take to the sergeant. Remember, this is the Doug Goodale gang. The sergeant has heard of them and knows how dangerous they are."

After Slocum had planted the bug in the cavalry sergeant's ear about how dangerous Goodale was, this ought to get the entire troop of horse soldiers riding out to capture the territory's most wanted outlaw. Slocum had convinced the sergeant that, since Sheriff Bullock had rounded up the Wall gang and broken the Bivens gang, the best way to maintain prestige was to go after Goodale.

The boy raced off to take the news to the cavalry, and Slocum strolled down the street toward the sheriff's office. General Adams would either take his men on a wild-goose chase and get them away from the stagecoach or he'd nab Goodale when he returned to the camp. Either way, Slocum was content.

"Where 'n the bloody hell have you been?" roared Seth Bullock when Slocum walked into the small jail. "I told everyone to be here an hour ago. The damn stagecoach's about ready to leave."

"Been out scouting all night long, sheriff," Slocum said. "I got good information. The Goodale gang's going to try to take the coach between Jenny's Stockade and Fort Laramie."

"How'd you come by this?" demanded Lowry.

Slocum silenced him with a cold look.

"I've been working the Cut-Off Trail, looking for spoor, and came across a dozen or so of the bastards," Slocum lied. "I couldn't take them all by myself, but I snooped and overheard their plans." He walked to a map nailed to the wall and stabbed down with his finger. "About here is where they're intending to take the stagecoach."

"Not as good a place as over at Cold Springs," said Bullock, stroking his chin.

"But Cold Springs is such a good spot they figured they'd get the coach *after* it left and you'd sent the posse on back to Deadwood. If they got the team switched at the depot in Cold Springs, nobody'd expect an attack later on."

"The cavalry would cut them to ribbons if they tried a robbery there. Fort Laramie's not more 'n twenty miles off," said Lowry.

Slocum just shrugged. He could argue, but he saw from the frown on Bullock's face that serious doubts were forming. Let the lawman come to his own wrong conclusions. The more Lowry argued against robbery along the Jenny's Stockade–Fort Laramie trail, the more the sheriff would favor it. Human nature being what it was, the sheriff might even give Slocum a bonus just to spite the insufferable Lowry.

"Sheriff, you can't listen to this yahoo. He's—"

"Shut up, Lowry. I think Slocum's on to something. Cold Springs is the best place for a robbery. The stagecoach team's tired from the pull down the Cut-Off Trail, the driver and guards are lookin' forward to a rest, and there are any number of places for an ambush nearby."

"Then he's a lyin' son of a bitch!"

"I said it was the best place—and the road agents know this is where we'll be on guard the most. The team and people in the stagecoach might be tired, but we're ridin' guard, too. We'd be ready for anything up to an army attack."

"Sheriff, he—" Lowry got no farther. Bullock cut him off with a wave of his hand.

"I got no reason not to believe him. The outlaws *know* this is where we'd have the strongest concentration of men. The stretch between Jenny's Stockade and Fort Laramie is isolated and the branching canyons give several places where they can swoop down, rob the coach, and be gone in a few minutes."

"So we're going to patrol that stretch of the trail?" asked Slocum.

"Reckon so. It won't matter much if you're wrong and the owlhoots do try to take the coach at Cold Springs.

General Adams has more than enough bluecoats to protect his precious U.S. Mail."

Slocum saw that the seeds of duplicity he had planted were sprouting everywhere. Bullock was a hero in Deadwood for bringing in the Wall gang with hardly a struggle. The sheriff wasn't risking much letting General Adams guard the stagecoach at Cold Springs—or so he thought. Bullock hoped to be able to nab another band of highwaymen and look even better in the townspeople's eyes.

He just didn't know that the cavalry was going off to stop Goodale before he could strike and that they'd be miles and miles from Cold Springs. Slocum kept from puffing up with pride at how well his scheme was working. The cavalry wasn't going to be at Cold Springs and neither was Sheriff Bullock's posse. Goodale would have easy pickings.

And Slocum intended to pick Doug Goodale's bones clean after the robbery.

"Let's get movin'. We got a long ways to go if we want to escort the coach down the Cut-Off Trail and then ride ahead and check out the Jenny's Stockade area," Bullock said.

"But sheriff," complained Lowry, "there's not enough of us to patrol the entire road. It's twenty miles or more between Jenny's Stockade and Fort Laramie."

"We can do it," the sheriff said positively. He turned in Slocum's direction and said under his breath, "You're not mistaken on this, are you?"

"All I know is what I overheard. They were talking hard about Jenny's Stockade," Slocum said.

"You're going to make chief deputy after this is over," Bullock said. "You're workin' out better'n any two of the others. You got brains and you know when not to use that six-shooter of yours. Those are rare commodities in these parts. Every damn hothead wants to draw first and think later." Bullock slapped him on the back and steered him toward the stable. Slocum hoped the stable hand had already gone to give General Adams the bogus message. He didn't want the boy bubbling over with enthusiasm about how he was helping the sheriff. Bullock need only ask one or two questions and he'd figure out what Slocum was up to.

Slocum breathed a sigh of relief when he saw that the towheaded boy was still out delivering the message. Slocum took the grain bag from his sorrel's nose and saddled her. He vaulted up and rode out, ducking slightly as he passed through the stable doors. Lowry was already outside. The deputy glared at him.

"I don't know what you're pulling, Slocum, but I intend to stick to you like glue. You might be in cahoots with them robbers." Lowry watched carefully for some reaction to his crude interrogation.

Slocum laughed and urged his horse past.

"Don't go thinking too much, Lowry," he said. "You'll hurt yourself with the unaccustomed work."

"You coward. You—"

"You boys get on over to the stage office. We'll escort the treasure coach out of town like we were an honor guard." Bullock herded his deputies into the street and formed them into a straggly column that would have made any horse trooper snicker. The sheriff seemed not to notice that some men hung back and others clustered close.

At the stage company office, Bullock dismounted from his big black stallion and talked with the balding, nervous stationmaster for several minutes. The driver of the treasure coach waited impatiently, barely keeping his team under control. Slocum saw there were six horses already in harness. The spirited animals jerked and strained against the leather, wanting to get started. Slocum thought he saw the profiles of a couple of passengers, but he couldn't be sure. They were braver or more desperate than the ordinary stagecoach passenger, he thought. The richest gold shipment just begged to be stolen.

Alongside the passengers inside the armored wagon sat two men, shotguns across their laps. If this was all the protection the stage line provided, Doug Goodale would have no trouble at all taking the gold at Cold Springs. Even with the iron sheets giving protection, two men wouldn't be able to withstand the attack Goodale was likely to mount. Slocum wasn't kidding himself that Goodale would have only McLaughlin and the dim-witted miner with him.

Glorieta had inadvertently mentioned the name Spear, and there were probably four or five other outlaws who'd be riding with Goodale.

Slocum remembered the last time he had been in the outlaw's camp, too. He had heard hoofbeats leaving the area. It didn't take much imagination to believe the horse belonged to one of Goodale's henchmen.

"Men, there's some problem," said Bullock. "There's been a ruckus down the street that is of some concern to the stationmaster. Seems there's not enough room in the coach for all the cargo and he's afeared someone will try to take it here in Deadwood." Bullock scratched his chin, studied the eight deputies, and then pointed. "I want you and you to stay around and watch things for the stationmaster. I thought we'd patrolled Deadwood up real good last night and got most of the troublemakers run out, but it's not workin' out that way this morning. Go find a pair of drunk owlhoots named Morgan and Maier. They been makin' noises about robbin' the depot."

Slocum watched as the two deputies indicated by Bullock turned their ponies and headed back into town. That cut the number in the posse down to seven—and Slocum had to subtract himself from that number, too. Six men intent on preventing the Deadwood Treasure Coach from being robbed. And one damned sure it was going to be seized.

"We've got our work cut out for us now, men," Bullock said. "Seven men along the Jenny's Stockade–Fort Laramie road is spreadin' us mighty thin."

"Cold Springs is where they're going to try to rob the stagecoach," grumbled Lowry. No one paid him any attention. Slocum heaved a sigh of relief at this.

"Three of you on one side of the coach and the rest on the other. I'll lead the parade out of town," Bullock said.

Slocum almost laughed at the festive atmosphere. People on the sidewalks stopped and waved. He waved back when he saw the blond stableboy outside the general store, holding a long stick of peppermint candy. He had received part of his reward for the information about the Goodale gang.

The sportive air died when the stagecoach rolled out of

town and started down the Cut-Off Trail. Everyone remembered there had been eleven other robberies along this road in the past month—and Slocum hoped that some other gang didn't try to make it an even dozen before Goodale struck at Cold Springs.

16

"We can split off here," called Sheriff Bullock. He pointed up a branching canyon that led back into the Black Hills. "We can rejoin the stagecoach after the team change at Cold Springs."

"Wait a goldanged minute!" cried the driver. The short man fought to rein in his struggling horses. The grade was steep, and it was best that they keep moving to prevent the heavily laden wagon from rolling backward down the hill. The horses weren't cooperating, and the stagecoach's brake squealed loudly in protest of the driver's foot against it. "Where the Sam Hill are you going? You got this here stagecoach to protect from thieves. We're carryin' damn near five hundred pounds of gold! And that's not counting the cavalry payroll and the two U.S. Mail pouches crammed in under it all. You can't leave us be. There's outlaws working this road!"

"You'll be safe enough, Big Gene," Bullock said. "We're going to stop the road agents *before* they try to hold you up. You're going to remember this trip as the easiest you ever drove."

"I want protection. I sure as hell don't see them bluecoats. Don't know where they got off to, but I'm not lettin' the seven of you ride off and leave us to the mercy of the bandits." The driver stood up; his bandy legs bowed but his shoulders were firm with resolve. He flicked the long leather whip in his hand and sent it curling out to crack loudly just under Bullock's nose.

"Do that again, friend, and I'll see you in jail for assaulting a peace officer." Bullock sat astride his huge black stallion with his hand resting on his six-shooter. He meant business and the driver saw it. Big Gene cooled off a mite but wasn't totally repentant.

"Better in jail than in one of them graves," he groused. The short stagecoach driver pointed to a series of the nameless graves that were the most prominent feature along the Cut-Off Trail.

"Get moving," Bullock ordered. "The cavalry is waiting for you and we'll be ready on the other side of Cold Springs with prisoners."

"Yeah," called one of the guards inside the coach, pushing aside a dangling iron sheet. "Where *is* General Adams? I thought he was supposed to ride along with us, too."

"I don't know where he got off to," said Bullock. "He can do as he sees fit to protect his mail and the payroll. I'm entrusted with seeing that this here stage gets out of Dakota Territory and on its way to Cheyenne. Now shut up and let me do my job."

"The hell I'll shut up," snapped the driver. "I've got half a mind to turn this rig around and go back to Deadwood. They might fire me, but I wouldn't be dead *and* robbed."

"If you had half a mind, you'd double your intelligence," grumbled Bullock. He rode closer and looked up at the stage driver. "Get on out of here right now. There's no danger until after Cold Springs, and that's where we're going. We can prevent those road agents from even attemptin' a holdup."

"Stay with the coach and you can be sure you'll be on hand when they do," the driver shot back. Big Gene sat down heavily on the hard plank seat and laid the blacksnake whip down at his feet in the driver's box. The look he shot the sheriff was enough to turn lesser men to stone. Seth

Bullock ignored it and waved the heavily laden stagecoach on up the steep hill.

The sheriff wheeled his horse about and led the way down the branching canyon. Slocum had no idea where this went, but it didn't matter. The posse was going away from the golden treasure trove and giving Doug Goodale that much better chance to steal the load. Slocum pulled his watch from his vest pocket and did some quick calculations.

If he stayed with the posse for another three hours, then slipped away and rode for Cold Springs, he ought to reach the way station just in time to trail Goodale after the robbery. It shouldn't take the outlaw more than fifteen or twenty minutes to pack the gold on whatever mules he had brought along for the task. Each animal ought to be able to carry about a hundred pounds.

"Five mules," Slocum mused.

"What's that?" growled Lowry. "What did you say?"

"Nothing," Slocum answered. He hadn't been aware that the deputy rode so close at his side.

"You said 'five.' What did you mean by that?"

"My lucky number," Slocum lied.

"Mules your lucky animal?" The sneer on Lowry's face made Slocum want to push his fist down the man's throat and rip out his lungs. He knew he couldn't turn his back on the treacherous deputy if they got into a shoot-out. Lowry was just as likely to gun down Slocum as he was to shoot at a highwayman.

Slocum turned away and went back to his hard thinking on times and distances and weights. Goodale and those with him would wear out their horses getting back to camp after the gold was securely hidden away. That gave General Adams the chance to capture the outlaw band with little effort. If she had any sense, Glorieta Zimmermann would be far away from the campsite by the time the general arrived with his bluecoats.

Slocum shook his head. He still couldn't decide whether Glorieta was in league with Goodale or not. She might have told him everything about the visit from the cavalry. If she had, it didn't make a difference to Slocum. Goodale would have his spare horses near where he stashed the gold and would escape from there.

Slocum would retrieve the horses the stableboy had left out on the trail just east of Cold Springs and use them to move the gold. He wouldn't have to deal with Goodale again. The outlaw would either be too busy with General Adams and his men or would be racing the wind to get out of Dakota Territory, secure in his mistaken belief that his gold was safely hidden.

They rode for another hour and then turned down a valley. At the far end of the once-green gorge Slocum saw a thin streamer of smoke rising from a fire.

"That there's Jenny's Stockade," said Bullock, seeing his interest. "They graze the entire area in the spring with cattle and some sheep. Now the land's not worth a bucket of cold spit. Too dry and the grass has turned brown."

The sere, deserted valley told Slocum that it was getting closer and closer to the vicious winter storms that would come roaring down out of Canada. He had to get the gold into a safe place before the weather turned on him. From the frigid bite in the air, he didn't think it would be long— maybe only a few days.

"Don't see any place nearby where the outlaws might set up an ambush for the stagecoach," Slocum said, speaking the obvious. "Where's Fort Laramie from here?"

"Back that way," Bullock said, pointing toward the other end of the valley.

"The stagecoach will come down that road?" Slocum yearned to get out his brass spyglass, but knew better than to give away his ownership of such a valuable tool. It might be useful later.

Bullock looked to where Slocum pointed. "The trail winds down the valley and then on to Fort Laramie. The road agents have any number of places where they can come into the valley and then get back into the hills."

"From this vantage point, we can see them if they so much as stir," Slocum said. He hadn't considered the possibility that Bullock knew of such a lookout. The sheriff would keep his posse here, waiting for the slightest hint of movement before sending his deputies out to investigate. Slocum had no chance to get away, retrace the rocky trail to Cold Springs, and find Doug Goodale.

"We surely can. No need to go traipsin' all over the landscape lookin' for those mangy cayuses," said Bullock. "Rest up and we'll take them for certain."

Slocum paced nervously, wanting to get away from the posse. He couldn't simply slip away, not with Lowry eyeing him like a buzzard considering his next meal. Now and again Slocum stopped his pacing and looked back toward Jenny's Stockade and the deserted trail wandering in from Cold Springs.

"You look like you're going to miss a train," said Lowry. "You keep looking at your watch every few minutes. There's nothing important happening, now is there?"

"We ought to have seen outlaws by now," said Slocum. "We ought to get out on patrol. We're missing something. I feel it in my bones."

Bullock came over when he heard Slocum complaining. The sheriff scratched his chin and said, "You don't reckon you might have been wrong about what you overheard?"

"I heard what I said," snapped Slocum. "They might have been talking about something else. It didn't sound that way and they surely did look like road agents to me."

"I haven't seen so much as a rabbit stirring out in the valley," said Bullock. "I think it might be time to ride for Cold Springs and rendezvous with the stagecoach. Big Gene wasn't too happy I decided to come on this wild-goose chase."

Slocum met the sheriff's gaze without flinching. "I heard men I took to be outlaws talking about doing a robbery on the Jenny's Stockade–Fort Laramie road. I don't know why they're not here."

"They're not gettin' ready," snarled Lowry, "because they're at Cold Springs waiting to rob the coach there."

"Lowry may be right—and so was Big Gene. Damn, I ought to have listened to him back at the first hill, but he made me so mad with that bullwhip of his." Bullock heaved a sigh, squared his shoulders, looked angrily at

Slocum, then shouted, "Mount up, men. We're ridin' to Cold Springs."

Slocum rode at the side of the posse, never quite able to fall back enough to elude Lowry. They rode steadily for an hour, made the bend in the road toward Cold Springs, and left the valley behind. The going got rocky again, and then they saw the way station sitting in a bowl at the bottom of the canyon. A grassy sward surrounded Cold Springs. In the spring it would be a dot of green amid the rocky Black Hills. Now the stage depot was a darker spot in the middle of dead brown grass.

"The coach hasn't made it up the last grade yet," said Bullock. "We're probably in time—if there's even going to be a robbery. We done good in running off most of the road agents. What we haven't arrested or spooked, Captain Crawford's probably lynched and General Adams has scared off."

"Where is the general?" asked a deputy. "I didn't see the cavalry back in town."

"They're out scouting the area," said Lowry, "like we should have been doing. But no, we go off and sit on our butts for a couple hours looking for road agents where there weren't none. It don't take a genius to know that was a piss-poor spot for any highwayman to try to waylay the stagecoach."

Slocum didn't answer the deputy's gibe. It wouldn't do any good to get into an argument with him. Any trouble now would only magnify in intensity later, just when Slocum intended to turn to smoke and float away on the wind.

"Sheriff, look!"

The warning wasn't needed. The sounds of gunfire echoed across the valley. Seth Bullock let out a howl of anguish when he realized his reputation was at stake and put his spurs to his horse's flanks. The powerful animal bolted. The sheriff held on grimly, expecting his posse to follow. Slocum started his sorrel after the sheriff, not caring what happened to Lowry. Slocum had to get across the valley, past the Cold Springs depot, and get Goodale's trail before the outlaw vanished with the gold. He had struck just before the stagecoach reached the way station, something Slocum had feared. It would take hard riding to just get to the scene of the crime.

The posse pounded hard to reach the stagecoach. Even before they got close enough to do anything about road agents, Slocum saw the bandy-legged Big Gene standing up in the driver's box and waving his arms wildly.

Big Gene reached down and picked up his bullwhip and cracked it louder than any gunshot. Slocum wondered if this wasn't what they had heard earlier. Goodale might have been able to pull off the robbery without firing a shot. The treasure coach had been moving slowly to get up the final grade before Cold Springs. Big Gene's concentration would have been on controlling the six-horse team. The guards might have been tired, just as Slocum had anticipated. Their attention would have been focused forward, rather than to the sides or rear where an attack was most likely to have come from.

"Where the hell have you been?" came Big Gene's outraged cry. "They took us slicker'n snot. They took us and we didn't even have a chance to fire a single damned shot!"

"Where is General Adams and his cavalry? He was supposed to be guarding the stagecoach," asked Bullock.

"How the hell should I know? I ain't seen hide nor hair of any bluecoat since Deadwood. They all left. I thought they was watchin' the road for highwaymen. Hell, I thought *you* were, too!"

Big Gene cracked his long whip again, this time in frustration.

"Anyone hurt?"

"Those two good-for-nothings the stage line's got inside the coach giving us protection tossed their shotguns out at first sight of a six-shooter stuck in their faces. No shots were fired." Big Gene cracked his whip again. Slocum was sure now that this was the sound they had heard and not gunfire.

"Where did they rob you?" demanded Bullock.

Slocum dismounted and went to the coach. He pushed

aside a heavy dangling iron plate. There weren't any fresh scratches on it or evidence of anything more powerful than a thorny bush rubbing along it. The driver's recollection of the robbery must have been exact. No shot had been fired at the stagecoach or, Slocum thought taking a deep breath, from inside. The heavy odor of gunpowder would have clung to the coach's interior if anyone had gotten the gumption to fight. The guards had simply surrendered and not put up a fight.

"Glad to see you boys," one guard said. He jumped down. The other followed, leaving the two passengers inside the coach. "They took us clean before we knew what was happening."

The other's head bobbed up and down in silent agreement. Slocum saw that the second man's jeans were stained in the front from where he had gotten mighty scared.

"They got all the gold. Loaded six damned mules with it and took off. And their leader made a big point out of stealin' the mail pouch. He downright laughed when he stole it." Big Gene paused to get his breath, then added, "They got the cavalry payroll, too. That they deserve. Where the hell was General Adams? What are we payin' them pissants for, anyway?"

Bullock and the driver started arguing again. Slocum pushed past the two guards and poked his head into the passenger compartment of the huge stagecoach.

"What about you folks?" he asked. "You all right?"

"I am, sir," came a deep voice. "But the lady's real frightened. Nothing like this has ever happened to her, I do imagine."

Slocum didn't bother with the man. His eyes fixed firmly on the woman. Glorieta Zimmermann sat with her hands in her lap, tears streaming down her face.

"He left me," she said in a voice so low only Slocum could hear. "The son of a bitch took the gold and left me!"

17

John Slocum looked back over his shoulder, expecting
Lowry to be standing there, listening to every single word
Glorieta Zimmermann said. The deputy was talking with a
guard and only occasionally glanced in Slocum's direction.

"What happened?" Slocum asked in a low voice. The
other passenger, a tall, thin man, moved to get down from
the compartment. Slocum let him pass, then jumped into the
stage and sat beside Glorieta. "Goodale got the gold and
then what happened?"

"He double-crossed me!" She didn't quite wail but she
came close enough for Slocum to know Glorieta restrained
herself only by sheer force of will. She was angry and
hurt—and betrayed. She had intended to double-cross him
and go riding off with Goodale. That much was apparent.
And now Goodale had turned the tables on her.

"How many men did Goodale have with him? It was more
than just McLaughlin and the dim-wit miner."

"Spear was with him, Spear and three others. There were
seven all told, counting Doug. I knew about Spear, but
he never mentioned the others. How dare he do this! He
double-crossed me!"

"Did you tell Goodale about General Adams and the cavalry going to the camp?"

Her head went up and down twice in a barely perceptible movement. A strand of her dark hair poked out from under the simple brown gingham bonnet she wore. Slocum wondered if there had ever been a more beautiful woman. Or one more confused about her loyalties.

"Then Goodale isn't going back to the camp," Slocum said, more to himself than Glorieta. That didn't matter. Goodale would be stashing the gold now and getting ready for a quick ride out of Dakota Territory. Slocum lifted Glorieta's chin with his finger and looked into her blue eyes. She flinched away.

"I'm sorry, John. I didn't mean to betray you. He—he's so convincing and you weren't there much and—"

"Never mind that. What the hell were you doing on the coach?"

"Doug said it was part of the plan." She lifted her clutch purse. From the weight inside, Slocum guessed she had a small pistol. When she opened it he saw the derringer. "I was supposed to take care of the guards inside if they tried to put up a fuss."

Slocum appreciated the cleverness of this scheme. It insured a quick and easy robbery. General Adams would be on a wild-goose chase. Bullock and his posse would be patrolling a stretch of road where no one in their right mind would ever try to hold up a stagecoach, and Glorieta would get the drop on the only two men capable of putting up any resistance. It was a damned good plan.

And it had worked. Slocum cursed his bad luck in having Bullock decide to sit and watch, rather than actively patrol the Jenny's Stockade–Fort Laramie road. He hadn't been able to get away in time to see the actual robbery. He only hoped that following Goodale wouldn't be hard.

He closed his eyes and tried to imagine how he could do it with the entire posse hot on his heels. It didn't seem to be an easily solved problem.

"What's going on in there?" came Lowry's querulous voice.

"I'm finding out what happened," Slocum shot back.

"We're gettin' ready to ride. Get your ass out here and into a saddle," ordered Lowry.

"I'll have to go," Slocum said. "If you'd thrown in with me, we'd be splitting the gold. Now, it doesn't look as if either of us will see so much as a speck of gold dust."

"I'm sorry, John. I am!"

"No time for that now," he said, already making plans. "You get on down to the Cold Springs depot and wait for for me there. When I finish with Goodale, I'll be back for you."

"But the gold!"

Slocum shrugged, as if telling her that wasn't important right now. Glorieta accepted the gesture and lightly touched his arm. It was all there could be between them with Lowry standing just outside.

Slocum's foot had hardly hit the ground when he was plotting on getting back the gold Goodale had stolen. Goodale had six others with him. Unless Slocum missed his guess, McLaughlin and the miner were already history. He couldn't see a slick operator like Doug Goodale splitting the take with them.

And what about the others, the ones he had kept hidden from Slocum? Glorieta had mentioned Spear several times. He was Goodale's right-hand man. The others might be remnants of his old gang who had tagged along when Goodale moved north. Taking on five dangerous outlaws wasn't something that pleased Slocum, but it had to be done.

He climbed into the saddle just as Bullock began his little speech. "We've been snookered, men. They robbed the coach just at the top of the grade. Nobody knows where the cavalry boys got off to, but they're not around here. We're on our own tracking the outlaws down."

"How many are there?" asked a deputy, nervously counting the posse and coming up short by several dozen.

"The best Big Gene can figure, there was seven of them. They loaded the gold onto mules and took off in that direction." Bullock pointed north, but the vagueness robbed it of any real meaning. "Following them ought to be easy.

Taking them into custody is going to be something of a chore. They're mean ones."

"Were they the Doug Goodale gang?" asked Lowry.

"There's ample reason to think that. We done jailed the Bivens and Wall gangs. Who else is left in Dakota Territory with enough balls to pull off a robbery like this?"

Slocum remained silent. He had been the one to draw attention to the Doug Goodale gang. No one had considered them a serious threat until he started warning the sergeant and others about them. At his left, Lowry glared at him, his mind turning over all the possibilities. Slocum wondered how long it would take the feral deputy to decide Slocum had been a member of the gang. He had been poking around and making enough trouble. This accusation didn't take any huge leap of faith to make. Slocum hoped the sheriff didn't take it into his head to think on it a bit. Seth Bullock needed a scapegoat and who better to pin this disaster on than his newest deputy.

"An easy trail, men," Bullock called out. He had to slow his breakneck speed because his stallion was tiring rapidly. Slocum took a few minutes and got his own bearings as the sheriff slowed them to a walk. The horses he had the stableboy bring out weren't too far away. He hoped that Goodale had stashed the gold fast and then cut and run. If he hadn't, they would have to chase the outlaw down.

Slocum didn't think Doug Goodale was so stupid as to think he could make it out of Dakota Territory with a train of pack mules so loaded down with gold that their legs bowed. The original plan had been a good one; nobody could hope to escape a posse hot on his trail.

"There," said Bullock. "There's where they went. Look at that." The sheriff dropped to the ground and hefted a small gold bar that had slipped out of a pack.

Slocum frowned when he saw it. Goodale wasn't this careless. When he packed, he made sure everything was secure. If the robbery had taken place under poor circumstances, Slocum might have believed the gold ingot was left behind in the confusion of the getaway. But the robbery of the Deadwood Treasure Coach had gone flawlessly. Not a single shot had been fired and the getaway was slick as a whistle. That could only mean that the gold was dropped on purpose to draw off pursuit.

"Enough resting," said Bullock. "We've got road agents to catch."

"String 'em up," grumbled Lowry. He turned and looked squarely at Slocum when he added, "String *all* of them up from the nearest cottonwood."

"Sheriff, this isn't the right trail," Slocum said. "Why would they leave behind this much gold unless it was to throw us off?"

"They got careless," Bullock said, hardly listening. Slocum was no longer a valued advisor since he had been proven wrong about the robbery. Slocum saw that all he could do was ride along and look for an opportunity to get away from the posse. Doug Goodale had left this gold behind in the same way a crooked miner salted his own mine. This was a lure, not a meaningful signpost.

Slocum began to doubt his own judgment when they got to the top of a rise and looked down into another valley. The dust being kicked up by the riders below showed a goodly number of men. And the speed at which they traveled told Slocum they were burdened heavily.

"That's them, men," said Bullock. "Check your side arms and get those rifles loaded. This one's going to be a fight to the death. Nobody's givin' up five hundred pounds of gold without one whale of a fight!"

Slocum rode along, not wanting to get involved. He couldn't believe Goodale had been this stupid. He had left a trail a blind man could find in a blizzard and now he was trotting along as if he didn't have a care in the world. The posse had enough firepower with it to make things very hot for the outlaw leader.

Why? Slocum kept turning over the question in his mind. It made no sense that Doug Goodale would do what he had seemed to. A perfect robbery and a completely idiotic escape.

As the posse rode closer, Slocum got a better look at the men they were following. He saw only five riders and five mules. The spirited pursuit brought one rider around. Slocum saw him jerk at another's sleeve and shout at the others. The road agents knew they were being hounded by Seth Bullock now.

"They're headin' for the trees," Lowry called. "We can cut them off. Then we can kill the bastards where they stand!"

Slocum saw that Lowry's tactic wasn't going to work. The robbers had just enough of a warning to make it impossible. They got to the edge of the stand of trees just as Bullock galloped forward, his six-shooter blazing. The six bullets he scattered around didn't hit anyone, but they spooked the road agents' horses enough to keep them from making a clean break into the forest.

"Give it up!" shouted Bullock. "We'll string you up from the trees if you don't surrender. We got you red-handed!"

"The hell you say!" came the answer. Close on the heels of the words came a volley of bullets. Leaden bees buzzed past Slocum. He ducked low. The men in the forest had their rifles out and were able to take careful aim. He veered to the left and dropped behind a large rock.

"Coward!" cried Lowry. The man seemed to have lost all fear. He charged directly into the woods, his pistol firing sporadically. Slocum thought he heard the hammer fall on a dud round. That reduced Lowry's chances of getting back alive by one.

For his part, Slocum wouldn't be sorry to see the deputy gunned down. But there was a god who protected drunks and fools. Lowry swung around and came galloping back, unscathed.

"We got 'em pinned down," he gloated. "All we need to do is smoke 'em out. They can't last forever in there."

"Don't go settin' the woods on fire again," cautioned Bullock. Slocum heard the irritation in the sheriff's voice. Lowry must have done something similar before Slocum came along.

Slocum pulled his rifle out and laid it across the top of the rock. From this range he didn't think he would have any trouble picking off the road agents one by one.

But he worried a mite about it. He hadn't seen Doug Goodale.

"There's five of them in there," Lowry went on. "I scouted them out. They got mules loaded down with the gold, too. We got 'em all!"

Slocum didn't correct the deputy. Let him think they had rounded up all the robbers. He sighted along his Winchester and squeezed back on the trigger. The recoil was satisfying against his shoulder, and he knew he had made a good shot. The anguished yelp from the woods was added proof of his aim.

"Good going," congratulated Bullock. He stared at Slocum in real admiration. "You can really use that rifle."

Slocum said nothing. During the war he had been a sniper. Most of his shots had been under adverse conditions and at ranges five times this one. He just had to argue with himself over killing the men in the forest or letting the sheriff take them alive. He didn't need one of them accusing him of being in on the robbery.

"There's one. He's making a run for it!"

Slocum wasn't even sure who cried out the warning. Seven rifles turned and fired as one. The man fell backward off his horse and lay faceup on the ground just outside the edge of the woods. Slocum recognized McLaughlin from his checked shirt. This took some of the pressure off him. He didn't think the hard rock miner Goodale had recruited would be able to identify him. The miner had always been on guard duty and had never seen him when he rode into the outlaw camp.

"You can't get away. We'll give you a fair trial if you give up now without any more fuss!"

Sheriff Bullock's words fell on deaf ears. Slocum rose up and aimed when he saw a squat figure come from the woods. He hesitated just for a moment, wondering what the man was doing. He fired just as the miner reared back and let loose a bundle of dynamite.

The miner was dead by the time he hit the ground. Slocum barely had time to duck back before the four sticks of dynamite exploded. Rock and debris rained down. Two of the deputies were dead and another two were injured. Slocum cursed his bad luck when he saw that Lowry wasn't one of the dead or injured. The man had turned into a juggernaut of destruction, walking through terror and seemingly thriving on it.

"I'll flush those sons of bitches out," Lowry declared. He ran through the cloud of dust kicked up by the dynamite and vanished.

Slocum began edging around the rock and going toward the south end of the woods, intending to cut off anyone escaping in that direction. From the intensity of the gunfire, no one might be able to get out alive.

When he had reached a decent vantage point, he settled down to wait. From his perch in the limbs of a cottonwood getting ready to drop its yellow leaves for the autumn, he was able to see the road agents clearly. It was as he had suspected. There were only five men. Of Doug Goodale he saw no trace. Slocum guessed that a rollcall of the outlaws would also show Spear to be missing.

The mules brayed and kicked, trying to get away from the gunfire. Slocum watched carefully. A slow smile crossed his lips. Goodale had been busier than a bee. One mule threw off its load. Worthless rock cascaded to the ground. Slocum didn't doubt for an instant that the other mules were similarly laden.

Somehow, Goodale and Spear had given these feckless fools slag and kept the gold. The dropped ingot not only marked the trail these five had taken, it would convince the law that they had the stolen gold. No matter how much they protested, no jury would believe that they weren't the sole culprits in the crime.

Another mule bucked and got free of its load. Slocum saw the glint of gold—more flash to convince the men that they carried the loot. Slocum doubted more than a few dollars' worth of gold was in the packs.

"Give up," shouted Seth Bullock. "We got you men right and proper."

Someone shot at him. Slocum aimed and squeezed. His round took off the outlaw's hat. The man jerked around as if the hot lead had ripped through his flesh. When he saw that the posse had the grove surrounded, he dropped his rifle and raised his hands.

The other road agents quickly surrendered, too. They saw that they had no chance to get away alive. Their chances with a lynch mob might not be any greater, but they'd stay alive a few days more.

"That's it, men," called out the sheriff. "Let 'em surrender. Don't gun 'em down now."

Slocum guessed Bullock was looking directly at Lowry when he gave that command. No one else in the posse was anywhere near as trigger-happy. Slocum jumped down from the tree and went to the mules. He spent a few minutes gentling them, then began digging through the packs. Tailings from a played-out mine dribbled from the packs and formed a small hill at Slocum's feet. The more he worked, the more slag he got. From the five mules he pulled out only ten gold bars. Each had been carefully placed on top of the pack so that anyone making a casual inspection would believe there was lots more beneath.

"This is it?" asked Bullock, astounded at the paucity of the gold recovered. "There's not twenty thousand dollars' worth here. The stagecoach was loaded with almost a quarter million in gold!"

"I make it to be twenty-six thousand, sheriff," said one of the wounded deputies. He propped himself against a rock, his face pale. "I used to work in an assay office. They either hid the bulk of the gold or they didn't rob this from the treasure coach."

Bullock spun and faced one of the outlaws. "Where's the rest, you mangy cayuses! Tell me or I'll string you up by your ears."

"But—we—they double-crossed us. They took the gold and left us with shit!"

"Don't lie to me," roared Bullock. "I want the truth!"

Slocum knew the truth. Doug Goodale had the remainder of the gold. Damned near a quarter million dollars' worth, just for him and Spear. And considering Goodale's actions so far, his right-hand man Spear might be lying facedown in a gully somewhere, a bullet in the back of his head. That much gold proved a mighty powerful lure.

Slocum slipped away from the posse. Let them question the survivors of the Deadwood Treasure Coach robbery as much as they wanted. He knew where the false trail had started, and he knew who he had to find.

And Slocum also knew the golden prize that would be his when he finished with Doug Goodale.

18

"Where do you think you're going?" came the cold words. Slocum froze in his tracks. He hadn't been paying enough attention to Lowry. The deputy stood directly behind him. The hair rose on the back of Slocum's neck. This told him there was a gun aimed squarely at his spine. He didn't know how he had come by this sixth sense, but he always believed its message. So far, it had kept him alive.

"I was just going off to take a leak," Slocum lied.

"Hold your water. We got more trackin' to do," said the deputy in a nasty voice. Slocum turned slowly and found that once more his sixth sense was right. Lowry stood with his six-shooter drawn, cocked, and aimed at Slocum.

"You don't need to keep pulling your gun on me," Slocum said, level and cold. "It's making me mighty nervous. And when I get nervous, someone usually dies."

Lowry sneered at him. The gun never wavered. "I can't pin this robbery on you, but you know more'n you're lettin' on. I feel it down deep in my gut."

"That's just the lousy coffee you fix eating away at your stomach," said Slocum. "I don't think you've got any guts. You're all the time sneaking up behind me. I don't think you're anything more than a coward and a backshooter."

155

"You—" Lowry lifted the six-shooter just enough to show that Slocum had goaded him into firing.

The report echoed through the Black Hills, but the bullet sailed harmlessly into the air. Sheriff Bullock had come up behind Lowry and jerked the gun away from its target just in time. Slocum had been watching and had played a dangerous game. He was glad that Bullock had decided not to let one of his deputies gun down another. Slocum was fast, but he could never have drawn, aimed, and fired before Lowry squeezed off a round.

"What the hell are you doing?"

"He was tryin' to sneak away, sheriff," said Lowry. Bullock handed him back his six-shooter but stood between his two deputies. "He's in cahoots with them. I know it."

"There's nothing to make me think that," said Bullock, but Slocum heard the slight quaver in the sheriff's voice. He was beginning to have his doubts.

"He led us up to Jenny's Stockade for nothing," Lowry said. "That ought to prove he's in with them. There weren't any outlaws talkin' about robbin' the stagecoach there. He made it all up just to get us away from the treasure coach."

"We'll talk about this later. Get mounted, Lowry. We got more road agents to track down." Bullock turned to Slocum and eyed him up and down. "And I just don't know what to make of you. I thought you were a straight shooter, but I'm gettin' some doubts now."

"I want what you do, sheriff," Slocum said in all sincerity. The difference was that Bullock wanted to recover the stolen gold to return it to the Gilmer, Saulsbury, and Patrick Stage Company. Slocum wanted it for himself.

"There's something going on here, and I'll get to the bottom of it when we get back to Deadwood," the sheriff said. "I don't want you and Lowry lockin' horns. Do I make myself understood?"

"You surely do, sheriff," Slocum said. He didn't see any way out of riding along with the posse. He cursed silently as he mounted and started back along the trail they had just traversed. The stolen gold was buried somewhere near Cold Springs. Slocum knew it. The more time he spent with the posse, the less time he had to find Goodale's trail.

Even as the need for haste in getting after Goodale pressured him, something else nagged at the back of his mind. He tried to corner the random thought, but it eluded him again and again. He was missing something. But what was it?

They rode back to the spot where the gold bar had been found. Bullock looked at the three prisoners and the two dead road agents stretched over their pack mules, then took inventory of the men with him in the posse. Slocum prayed that he'd be told to escort the prisoners back. If Bullock sent him alone, the road agents would get a head start out of Dakota Territory. If the sheriff sent someone else with him, he could either slip away and leave the other deputy with the chore of getting the prisoners back to Deadwood, or he could just gun the other deputy down. This thought appealed mightily to him if Lowry was sent along.

"You and you," Bullock said, volunteering two of the other deputies, the ones injured in the shoot-out. "Get these owlhoots back to town and be sure they're safe and sound behind bars when we get back. And be sure Doc Magee looks at your wounds."

Slocum didn't let his disappointment show. Bullock hadn't chosen him. Neither had the sheriff chosen Lowry. That left a nasty thorn in Slocum's side.

"There's not as many of us to hunt down the other crooks," Bullock said after the two injured deputies started off with their prisoners, "but we got the best trackers." He looked squarely at Slocum. "You got to prove yourself to me after that fiasco back between Jenny's Stockade and Fort Laramie. Don't screw this one up."

Slocum knew better than to protest. His chance would come sooner or later. He just had to be ready to take it.

Slocum scoured the area where they had found the dropped bar of gold and finally saw two faint trails leading off in different directions. Either might be Doug Goodale. The other must be his cohort Spear. But which was which? Slocum couldn't tell.

"There," said Lowry, looking over his shoulder. "I see trampled brush and there's a shiny nick on a rock. Fresh. Within a day. Someone else rode this way not too long ago."

"I see it," Slocum said, angry that Lowry had forced his hand. This trail was the one they had to follow. It might be Goodale's. If it was, Slocum knew he might never get the gold. Goodale would have hidden it and would trade the location for his freedom.

He stood and shook his head. The same thing might happen with Spear. He had never met the man and didn't know anything about him. But if he and Goodale were willing to double-cross five others—seven, if Slocum counted himself and Glorieta Zimmermann—the man was capable of damned near anything.

"One man, that direction," he said, pointing where Lowry was already looking. "I can't say it was another of the road agents, but it's pretty likely."

"How many pack animals?" asked Bullock. "There must be a half dozen or more if they're carryin' the gold that wasn't sent with the other five outlaws."

"Don't see evidence of more than one rider on a shod horse," Slocum said honestly. "We can keep looking."

"We'll follow this trail for a spell," Bullock decided. He wanted a quick end to this. If he didn't capture all the robbers and recover the gold, the stage line would have his hide nailed to the outhouse door and the people of Deadwood might just string him up.

Slocum only wanted to get the hell away from the posse. Every second he stayed, he came closer to getting a bullet in the back from Lowry or arousing Seth Bullock's suspicions. Even worse, the notion was slowly twisting around in his mind that he had better leave Dakota Territory now and forget about the gold. That was the prudent thing. That was the course of action that might save his neck from getting stretched if the lawmen got wise to him.

The lure of so much gold, though, held him like a chain.

They rode in silence, their horses tired from the day's travel. Slocum was the first to top the rise and the first to see the lone rider working his way up a steep path on the other side of the mountain.

Bullock's large stallion struggled up the slope and stopped next to Slocum's sorrel. The sheriff wiped sweat beading his forehead in spite of the brisk, cold wind whipping through the canyons of the Black Hills.

"There he is, sheriff," Slocum said. It took Bullock several seconds to find the mounted outlaw on the far side of the canyon.

"You got good eyes," the sheriff said. "How are we ever going to catch up with him? He's got an hour's head start on us. By the time we reach the bottom of the canyon and start up the far side, he'll be over the ridge and gone."

Slocum reached into his bedroll and pulled out the spyglass. He opened it and held the tube up. It took several seconds of fiddling to bring the distant rider into focus. When the red-check-shirted rider came into view, Slocum heaved a sigh of relief. It wasn't Doug Goodale. It might be his henchman Spear or it might be someone else. But it wasn't Doug Goodale.

If the posse got the man alive, he wouldn't be able to tell of Slocum's involvement in the robbery. Slocum watched the rider for almost a minute, puzzling over the way the distant horse stepped so carefully. There might be a few pounds of gold in the man's saddlebags, but Slocum doubted it. He might not even be the road agent who had thrown in with Goodale.

"That's a mighty fancy eyepiece you got there," Bullock said in admiration. "Why haven't you used it before?"

"Didn't need to," Slocum said, not wanting to give away any advantage. Now he saw no way around it. Something that had been in the back of his mind for some time suggested the solution to the fleeing man on the other side of the canyon.

"Cut me some strips of rawhide, will you, sheriff?" Slocum dismounted and got his Winchester from its sheath. He levered in a round and dropped to the ground, the spyglass resting on top of the barrel. The sheriff and the others gathered around as Slocum fastened the spyglass to the rifle barrel. He rested the rifle in the notch of a low, sturdy shrub and peered through the eyepiece.

His first shot struck the mountainside a dozen feet below the rider. The man turned and looked around, startled. Slocum fired again, correcting for the distance. This shot fell only a few feet low. The third shot was luckier than it had any right to be at this distance.

The rider jerked around in the saddle, grabbed his leg, and almost fell from the saddle.

"You hit the son of a bitch!" crowed a deputy. "I never seen shootin' like that!"

"Got lucky," mumbled Lowry. "And we still don't have that owlhoot. We're miles from him."

"The bullet must have gone through his leg and into his horse," Slocum said. The horse wobbled and fell to one knee. He didn't much care for the notion of cutting a man's horse out from under him. Slocum often allowed as to how he usually preferred the man's mount to the man.

"Let's go get him," declared Bullock. "I never saw such shooting. Using that spyglass is a damned fine idea."

"Need a more powerful rifle," Slocum said. "A Sharps .69 with a tripod mount would do the trick."

They rode down the canyon and up the far side. By the time they reached the spot where the man's horse had died, it was twilight. The horse had been shot a second time, through the head. Slocum felt a bit of admiration for the horse's rider. He had done the right thing when he saw the horse was in misery.

"Fan out and find the bastard," ordered Bullock. "I want to know where he stashed that gold."

Slocum stood and waited, not knowing what to do. The trail back down the hill was steep, but he might be able to reach the canyon bottom before anyone missed him. He could follow the small stream there to a wider valley and from there—where would he go?

The lure of the gold was still too great for him to simply ride off. Good sense told him the bullion from the robbery was lost. Doug Goodale had hidden it and was on his way to Canada by now.

That thought rankled and did more to hold Slocum than simple greed. Letting Goodale win by double-crossing went against his grain.

"We found him, sheriff," came the call from up the narrow, rocky trail. "He's holed up behind some rocks."

"Let's flush our prairie chicken," Bullock said. Slocum followed, aware that Lowry's hot eyes watched him like a buzzard waiting for its dinner to die. Slocum hefted his Winchester, wondering how easy it would be to take out Lowry.

A bullet sent his hat sailing and put such speculation to rest. The hat blew backward, telling Slocum the man who had fired on him was upslope. He fell forward, the Winchester ready for action. A long tongue of yellow and orange flame licked out. Slocum pinpointed the source. The other deputy had been right about the outlaw's position.

"Getting him out in the open will be damned near impossible," Slocum said. "He's got a good field of fire."

"We can exhaust his ammunition," said Bullock.

"You mean we can let him fill us full of lead?"

"You got an attitude problem, Slocum." The sheriff turned back to the fight, sending a few rounds of his own singing off into the gathering night.

Slocum saw no way for them to get the man out.

"We know you robbed the treasure coach," shouted Bullock. "We got the others who helped you in custody. They're probably already safe in jail back in Deadwood. Give it up right now and you can have a hot meal tonight."

His only answer was a pair of deadly bullets, one of which missed his head by scant inches.

"Talking him down isn't working, sheriff," observed Slocum. "And we don't know how much ammo he's got. He might have enough for a siege."

"Food," grumbled Bullock. "Water. He'll run out of something sooner or later."

Slocum wasn't inclined to wait. The imagine of Doug Goodale making off with the gold burned like a hot fire in his guts. For every second they wasted taking this man out, Goodale was that much farther away with the gold. Slocum bent low and dodged to the side away from the sheriff. He had hoped that Lowry would think he was making a break for it. And he did. The deputy followed and drew heavy fire from above.

Slocum jerked the rifle to his shoulder and fired reflexively. The bullet found its mark. For the second time that day, he had made a miraculous shot. The outlaw slumped forward, his six-shooter slipping from nerveless fingers.

"You got him! You got him!" The others rushed forward. Slocum hurried forward, too, intending to put a bullet through the man's head if he tried to implicate him in the stagecoach robbery.

Unfocused eyes looked up. Slocum didn't know the man, but that didn't mean the man didn't know him.

"I've seen posters out on this one," said Bullock. "Name's Spear. That right? Are you Spear?"

"Yes, damn you to hell," came the weak voice.

"We got the other five. You double-crossed them. They didn't have but a tiny bit of the gold from the robbery. Where did you cache the rest of it? There must be well nigh five hundred pounds of gold bars still missing."

"I'll never tell you. Never." Spear gasped. Blood trickled from the corner of his mouth. Then he moved like a striking snake, catching everyone by surprise. He scooped up his fallen pistol and lifted it, the muzzle pointed squarely at Seth Bullock.

A loud report filled the still night air.

19

The six-shooter in Slocum's hand recoiled as he sent a round squarely through the outlaw's head. Spear's eyes opened in surprise, then his fingers loosened on the butt of his pistol. He fell forward, dead before his face crashed into the dust.

"Damnation," Seth Bullock said in a low voice, visibly shaken at the nearness to death. "He would have killed me dead." The sheriff turned and stared at Slocum. The smoking Colt told the entire story. Slocum had just saved his life.

"I owe you a debt of gratitude," Bullock said.

"You would have done the same for me," Slocum said. In a way he was glad it had worked out this way. Silencing Spear kept the man from ever revealing the true details of the treasure coach robbery.

"He musta buried the gold somewhere along the way, sheriff," said Lowry. He had quickly searched Spear's belongings and had found only a small pouch filled with gold dust. "We can't beat it out of him." The deputy looked down at Spear. The outlaw's corpse was beginning to stiffen. In another hour it would begin to decay and be fit only for drawing flies and buzzards. Lowry glanced over at Slocum as if accusing him of some perfidy.

"There's nothing more we can do now, men," said Bullock. "It's too danged dark to hunt for the stolen gold. Let's rest up tonight and get back to the hunt tomorrow morning." Slocum saw the way the sheriff's hand shook. The close brush with death had shaken him more than he wanted anyone to know.

"Mind if I bury the varmint?" Slocum asked.

"What? No, go on," said Bullock. "We're going to the stream at the bottom of the canyon to camp. Catch up with us when you're done."

Slocum nodded. The other deputies left. Lowry started to protest, then saw the look on Bullock's face and thought better of it. He sullenly went with the others. Slocum began digging and had a fair grave dug by the time the last of the posse had vanished back down the steep slope.

Rolling Spear into the grave, Slocum muttered, "I hope I find Goodale so he can join you in hell." Slocum finished the distasteful matter by stacking rocks on top of the body. It wouldn't keep a determined wolf or coyote from digging, but it would keep most of the carrion eaters away. Slocum hadn't known Spear. He might have been one son of a bitch, but he deserved at least this insignificant grave. Any man did.

Slocum sat on a rock and stared into the darkness for some time. He thought hard even as he listened for sounds of the posse. Over the rush of water along the valley floor he heard the neighing of horses and the boisterous talk of men relaxing after a danger-filled day. Coming to a decision, he heaved himself up and mounted his sorrel. The horse protested his weight. He patted the horse's strong neck and quietly calmed the animal.

"It'll be fine," he said softly. "All we have to do is take it easy. No hurrying in the dark along this path."

He guided the horse on up the mountainside rather than down to where Bullock and the others were camped. Slocum got to the top of the ridge and looked around. The cold wind blowing through the Black Hills chilled him, but he hardly noticed. Thoughts of gold warmed him.

He had considered the sorry situation from different directions and had come to the conclusion that the gold might still be his if a spot of luck came his way. After being burdened with Lowry's suspicions all day, he was about due for some good luck.

Meandering down the far side of the hill brought him to a road that led directly to Cold Springs. Spear had undoubtedly intended to go in the other direction, north to Canada. But Slocum wanted what Doug Goodale had buried.

The stagecoach way station was silent as Slocum rode up. He dismounted and took a quick look at the stars. He had been riding most of the night. The spinning heavenly clock told him it was almost four in the morning. He let his horse drink a mite from a watering trough and went to the depot door. He knocked lightly, not really wanting to disturb the station keeper.

"Who's there?" came the immediate question. "I got a shotgun here."

"I'm one of Sheriff Bullock's deputies," Slocum said. He touched the badge still hanging on his vest. He had intended to toss the bent star away but had forgotten. Now it might come in handy. "I need to know what happened to the passengers on the stagecoach."

The door opened a crack. A double-barreled shotgun poked out. Looking down its long blue length was a bleary, red-rimmed eye. Whatever the stationmaster decided, it didn't include blowing away his nocturnal visitor.

"You mean the ones on the Deadwood Treasure Coach? The one, the tall preacher man, went on to Cheyenne. The lady bought herself a buckboard and cut out for Deadwood."

"For Deadwood?" Slocum asked mildly. It didn't surprise him that Glorieta Zimmermann hadn't stayed with the coach. And it certainly pleased him that she had taken a buckboard. The double-crossing wasn't over yet. Not by a country mile.

"Reckon it was for Deadwood. She went back up the trail in that direction."

"Thank you, sir," Slocum said. "Much obliged, and sorry to have disturbed your sleep."

"What sleep? Who can get any shut-eye when there's road agents on the loose everywhere?"

"Who but the road agents themselves, eh?" he answered, thinking he wasn't getting much sleep himself. But the promise of riches kept him moving. Slocum mounted his protesting sorrel and started up the road. The bright stars provided just barely enough light for him to make out the ruts in the road and the thin-wheeled track left by Glorieta's buckboard. Even so, Slocum almost missed the spot where she had pulled off the road and headed across country.

He wanted to gallop after the fleeing woman, but couldn't risk missing another sudden change of direction in the dark. She had been traveling in daylight, and Slocum thought she knew exactly where she was going. He rode on slowly and came to an old mining road. He had to get down and study the ground closely. Squinting didn't help. Even lighting a lucifer failed to show what he was looking for. He couldn't make out the trail in the dim light. Even though it rankled him to waste time, Slocum waited until sunup to continue.

The going got easier then. Glorieta had stuck to the road. Slocum picked up his pace and by noon he found where Doug Goodale had buried the loot from the stagecoach robbery. Looking around, Slocum tried to piece it all together in his head.

"The five with their fake loads of gold must have gone that way," he said to himself, sighting through a low pass to the east. "And Spear kept on along this road, cutting back and heading to where Bullock finally caught him." Slocum couldn't figure out where Goodale had gone, but it hardly mattered.

From the look of the excavated shallow pit, nearly all of the five hundred pounds of gold had been buried here under a sparse layer of dirt. The five accomplices had little enough and all Spear had on him was a small pouch of gold dust. Slocum didn't think Goodale was any more likely to weigh himself down in his attempt to escape.

But the buckboard tracks continuing along the road were distinctive now. Glorieta had found the cache and had stolen all of Goodale's take from the robbery.

Slocum caught up with the fleeing woman just after two in the afternoon.

He sat, his leg curled across the saddle pommel, as he watched her try to get her exhausted team to pull harder up a small slope. She had worked them to the breaking point and would kill them soon enough. Slocum wiped the sweat from his forehead and replaced his hat. He made sure his Colt Navy was resting easy in its cross-draw holster, and only then did he urge his sorrel forward. He wasn't sure what reception he would get from Glorieta Zimmermann.

She heard his horse's hooves clacking against the rocky road and swung around in the buckboard's seat, hand flying toward her purse. He remembered the derringer she had hidden there. Slocum slowed and stayed just out of range of the short-barreled weapon. If she hit him at this range, it would be pure chance.

"Howdy, Glorieta. Quite a coincidence we'd meet on the same road, isn't it?"

"John!" The name escaped her lips like a frightened bird flying from a nest. He wasn't sure if it was fear or relief he saw in her. "My horses are stopping on me. I need to keep moving."

"Reckon so," he said. "That's a mighty heavy load you've got for such a light buckboard. Five hundred extra pounds? Or was it the six hundred pounds the sheriff claimed might be in the shipment?"

"Whatever are you—" She stopped when she realized she couldn't fool him. He knew exactly what she had under the black oilcloth in the back of the buckboard.

"John," Glorieta said, changing her tactics, "I didn't know how to get in touch with you. I thought you'd gone back to Deadwood. I—"

"None of that matters, Glorieta," Slocum said. He rode up and rested his right hand near his six-shooter, in case he needed it. He watched her carefully to be sure she didn't try pulling the derringer and drilling him with its large caliber bullet.

"Doug was double-crossing us. *Both* of us."

"I know. How did you know where he was going to hide the gold?"

Glorieta swallowed. She looked pale and desirable in the

early afternoon sunlight. Her hair gleamed a blue-black and her bright eyes shone feverishly.

"I told him you were sending General Adams to his camp. He laughed when I told him."

"He never intended to return there," Slocum said. He had already decided as much.

"But he didn't know I overheard him and Spear talking about where to bury the gold. They double-crossed the others, too. They're tricky, John. They wanted it all for themselves."

"Five hundred pounds of gold bars? Why not?" He wanted to examine the booty, but refrained. Turning his back on this woman wasn't smart.

"I wanted it all for you—for us," she pleaded. "Really. I overheard Goodale and Spear and knew I could get it."

Slocum didn't bother pointing out that she had plotted her own double-cross before Goodale had left her on the stagecoach. No one in this robbery had played square with anyone else.

"Let's get the wagon over under some trees and let the horses cool off," he said. "They've still got enough strength to get that far." He pointed to a stand of trees. Straining, he thought he heard a small stream bubbling nearby. Glorieta had damn near killed her horses in her desire to get away with the gold.

She drove silently, then jumped down. He saw that she kept her handbag with her. The derringer was still a dangerous factor between them.

Slocum dismounted and went to the rear of the buckboard. One edge of the oilcloth had come unfastened during her flight. He lifted it with his left hand and stared underneath at the gold. His heart raced at the sight he uncovered. Each small gold bar weighed twenty pounds and he counted twenty of them.

"There's almost a hundred pounds of gold dust, too," Glorieta said. "Doug didn't take hardly any with him."

"Neither did Spear," Slocum said.

"What? How do you know?"

"He's dead," Slocum said brutally. "The posse caught up with him."

"What of Doug?" Her voice betrayed her concern for the road agent. Slocum shook his head. Glorieta might actually be in love with the two-timing backshooter.

"Spear was alone."

"Doug's plan was to ride on down to Atlantic in Iowa, spend a few weeks there until the Deadwood sheriff got tired of hunting, then return for the gold."

"He'd go back to Iowa as a successful miner after telling everyone on this trip what a fine claim he was going to stake out," finished Slocum. "A good plan. Too bad you've taken his spoils from the robbery."

"Too bad neither of you is going to be able to spend a cent of it," came Lowry's cold voice from behind Slocum.

"Who?" started Glorieta. She was reaching for her derringer. This drew the deputy's fire.

Slocum had been coiled tighter than a spring, ready to draw and fire. He had been so sure the danger came from Glorieta that he hadn't heard Lowry sneak up behind. But his muscles exploded into action. His hand flashed to the ebony butt of his Colt Navy. He drew, cocked, and fired in a single smooth motion.

Even as Lowry stiffened and then sank bonelessly to the ground, Slocum heard Glorieta's moan of pain.

He swung around, his six-shooter ready to kill again.

She had dropped her derringer in the dust and was trying to pick it up awkwardly with her left hand. Slocum got to the pistol before she could retrieve it.

"I'll hang onto this." He pocketed the small pistol.

"My right arm. He shot me!"

"It's not too bad," Slocum said. He ripped open the cloth and saw a shallow groove across the woman's fine skin. "Let me scout around and be sure he was alone, then I'll clean it up."

"But John!"

Slocum was already out prowling. He found Lowry's horse. The man must have trailed him throughout the night and Slocum had never once caught sight of him. Lowry's talent in this area had brought him only death. His instincts as a lawman were good, but Slocum's reflexes had been better when it came down to the killing.

He returned to where Glorieta sat on the back of the buckboard, clutching her bleeding arm.

"I'm going to die from infection. It burns like fire."

"It'll be fine when we clean it." He led her to the small stream and cleansed the wound. It had bled enough to keep from becoming infected. He finished off by tying a long, thin piece of the woman's own skirt around the upper arm.

"It hurts, but not so much now that you're with me, John."

"Glad you feel that way. We'd better be on our way, though. Lowry might have been scouting for the sheriff and his posse."

"John, there's a fortune in that buckboard! Five hundred pounds of gold!"

"Not that much," Slocum said. He turned his back on Glorieta and returned to the buckboard. He touched the shiny gold bars with longing, but knew better than to even heft one. His greed would devour him as it had Glorieta and Doug Goodale. The heavy leather pouch containing the dust was enough for him.

He heaved it onto the ground and began transferring the smaller rawhide pouches inside to his saddlebags.

"What are you doing, John? There's no need to do this. We can get to Canada in a week. There's no need to—"

She saw him taking a pair of the gold bars. He buried them at the base of a large tree.

"I might be back this way sometime." He stood and brushed the dirt from his hands.

"I don't understand. We can go to Canada. We're rich!"

"Go to Canada," he said. "If you want, fetch the two gold bars I just buried. It'll weigh you down a considerable bit if you do." He mounted. His sorrel sagged slightly under the additional load. He had split the gold dust into equal portions and slung his saddlebags over the horse's back.

"Where are you going? You can't leave me!" Her blue eyes were wild with fear.

"I don't rightly know where I'm going, but it's not with you. There's no way I could ever trust you, Glorieta. Not after all that's happened."

"John!" She ran to him, but he pushed her away with his foot. There wasn't any place in his life for her.

He rode away, her pleas to stay falling on deaf ears. He had enough gold to keep him happy for a long, long time. As for Glorieta Zimmermann, she might be able to get out of Dakota Territory if she lightened her load in the buckboard. As it stood, the buckboard was too heavily overloaded for her to get more than a dozen miles before it broke down. A glance back over his shoulder convinced Slocum that she wouldn't get far. Glorieta had gone to the tree where he had buried the two bars and was digging them up.

With so much metal in her rickety buckboard, her horses would soon die of exhaustion. And Slocum didn't think Seth Bullock was the kind of man to give up the hunt for the stolen gold.

Slocum might not have been happy at the outcome of the Deadwood Treasure Coach robbery, but he was rich enough to dilute his sorrows. Maybe he could find suitable company to help spend his loot in Boise. Maybe in Salt Lake City. Maybe even in San Francisco. As long as it was far, far away from the likes of Glorieta Zimmermann and Doug Goodale.

GILES TIPPETTE

Author of the best-selling WILSON YOUNG SERIES, BAD NEWS, and CROSS FIRE is back with his most exciting Western adventure yet!

JAILBREAK

Time is running out for Justa Williams, owner of the Half-Moon Ranch in west Texas. His brother Norris is being held in a Mexican jail, and neither bribes nor threats can free him.

Now, with the help of a dozen kill-crazy Mexican *banditos*, Justa aims to blast Norris out. But the worst is yet to come: a hundred-mile chase across the Mexican desert with fifty *federales* in hot pursuit.

The odds of reaching the Texas border are a million to nothing . . . and if the Williams brothers don't watch their backs, the road to freedom could turn into the road to hell!

JAILBREAK
by
Giles Tippette

On sale now, wherever Jove Books are sold!

**Here is the first chapter
of this
new Western
adventure.**

At supper Norris, my middle brother, said, "I think we got some trouble on that five thousand acres down on the border near Laredo."

He said it serious, which is the way Norris generally says everything. I quit wrestling with the steak Buttercup, our cook, had turned into rawhide and said, "What are you talking about? How could we have trouble on land lying idle?"

He said, "I got word from town this afternoon that a telegram had come in from a friend of ours down there. He says we got some kind of squatters taking up residence on the place."

My youngest brother, Ben, put his fork down and said, incredulously, "*That* five thousand acres? Hell, it ain't nothing but rocks and cactus and sand. Why in hell would anyone want to squat on that worthless piece of nothing?"

Norris just shook his head. "I don't know. But that's what the telegram said. Came from Jack Cole. And if anyone ought to know what's going on down there it would be him."

I thought about it and it didn't make a bit of sense. I was Justa Williams, and my family, my two brothers and myself and our father, Howard, occupied a considerable ranch called the Half-Moon down along the Gulf of Mexico in

Matagorda County, Texas. It was some of the best grazing land in the state and we had one of the best herds of purebred and crossbred cattle in that part of the country. In short we were pretty well-to-do.

But that didn't make us any the less ready to be stolen from, it indeed that was the case. The five thousand acres Norris had been talking about had come to us through a trade our father had made some years before. We'd never made any use of the land, mainly because, as Ben had said, it was pretty worthless and because it was a good two hundred miles from our ranch headquarters. On a few occasions we'd bought cattle in Mexico and then used the acreage to hold small groups on while we made up a herd. But other than that, it lay mainly forgotten.

I frowned. "Norris, this doesn't make a damn bit of sense. Right after supper send a man into Blessing with a return wire for Jack asking him if he's certain. What the hell kind of squatting could anybody be doing on that land?"

Ben said, "Maybe they're raisin' watermelons." He laughed.

I said, "They could raise melons, but there damn sure wouldn't be no water in them."

Norris said, "Well, it bears looking into." He got up, throwing his napkin on the table. "I'll go write out that telegram."

I watched him go, dressed, as always, in his town clothes. Norris was the businessman in the family. He'd been sent down to the University at Austin and had got considerable learning about the ins and outs of banking and land deals and all the other parts of our business that didn't directly involve the ranch. At the age of twenty-nine I'd been the boss of the operation a good deal longer than I cared to think about. It had been thrust upon me by our father when I wasn't much more than twenty. He'd said he'd wanted me to take over while he was still strong enough to help me out of my mistakes and I reckoned that was partly true. But it had just seemed that after our mother had died the life had sort of gone out of him. He'd been one of the earliest settlers, taking up the land not long after Texas had become a republic in 1845. I figured all the years of fighting Indians and then Yankees and scalawags and carpetbaggers and cattle thieves had taken their toll on him. Then a few years back he'd been nicked in the lungs by a bullet that should never have been allowed to head his way and it had thrown an extra strain on his heart. He was pushing seventy and he still had plenty of head on his shoulders, but mostly all he did now was sit around in his rocking chair and stare out over the cattle and land business he'd built. Not to say that I didn't go to him for advice when the occasion demanded. I did, and mostly I took it.

Buttercup came in just then and sat down at the end of the table with a cup of coffee. He was near as old as Dad and almost completely worthless. But he'd been one of the first hands that Dad had hired and he'd been kept on even after he couldn't sit a horse anymore. The problem was he'd elected himself cook, and that was the sorriest day our family had ever seen. There were two Mexican women hired to cook for the twelve riders we kept full time, but Buttercup insisted on cooking for the family.

Mainly, I think, because he thought he was one of the family. A notion we could never completely dissuade him from.

So he sat there, about two days of stubble on his face, looking as scrawny as a pecked-out rooster, sweat running down his face, his apron a mess. He said, wiping his forearm across his forehead, "Boy, it shore be hot in there. You boys shore better be glad you ain't got no business takes you in that kitchen."

Ben said, in a loud mutter, "I wish you didn't either."

Ben, at twenty-five, was easily the best man with a horse or a gun that I had ever seen. His only drawback was that he was hotheaded and he tended to act first and think later. That ain't a real good combination for someone that could go on the prod as fast as Ben. When I had argued with Dad about taking over as boss, suggesting instead that Norris, with his education, was a much better choice, Dad had simply said,

"Yes, in some ways. But he can't handle Ben. You can. You can handle Norris, too. But none of them can handle you."

Well, that hadn't been exactly true. If Dad had wished it I would have taken orders from Norris even though he was two years younger than me. But the logic in Dad's line of thinking had been that the Half-Moon and our cattle business was the lodestone of all our business and only I could run that. He had been right. In the past I'd imported purebred Whiteface and Hereford cattle from up North, bred them to our native Longhorns and produced cattle that would bring twice as much at market as the horse-killing, all-bone, all-wild Longhorns. My neighbors had laughed at me at first, claiming those square little purebreds would never make it in our Texas heat. But they'd been wrong and, one by one, they'd followed the example of the Half-Moon.

Buttercup was setting up to take off on another one of his long-winded harangues about how it had been in the "old days," so I quickly got up, excusing myself, and went into the big office we used for sitting around in as well as a place of business. Norris was at the desk composing his telegram so I poured myself out a whiskey and sat down. I didn't want to hear about any trouble over some worthless five thousand acres of borderland. In fact I didn't want to hear about any troubles of any kind. I was just two weeks short of getting married, married to a lady I'd been courting off and on for five years, and I was mighty anxious that nothing come up to interfere with our plans. Her name was Nora Parker and her daddy owned and ran the general mercantile in our nearest town, Blessing. I'd almost lost her once before to a Kansas City drummer. She'd finally gotten tired of waiting on me, waiting until the ranch didn't occupy all my time, and almost run off with a smooth-talking Kansas City drummer that called on her daddy in the harness trade. But she'd come to her senses in time and got off the train in Texarkana and returned home.

But even then it had been a close thing. I, along with my

men and brothers and help from some of our neighbors, had been involved with stopping a huge herd of illegal cattle being driven up from Mexico from crossing our range and infecting our cattle with tick fever which could have wiped us all out. I tell you it had been a bloody business. We'd lost four good men and had to kill at least a half dozen on the other side. Fact of the business was I'd come about as close as I ever had to getting killed myself, and that was going some for the sort of rough-and-tumble life I'd led.

Nora had almost quit me over it, saying she just couldn't take the uncertainty. But in the end, she'd stuck by me. That had been the year before, 1896, and I'd convinced her that civilized law was coming to the country, but until it did, we that had been there before might have to take things into our own hands from time to time.

She'd seen that and had understood. I loved her and she loved me and that was enough to overcome any of the troubles we were still likely to encounter from day to day.

So I was giving Norris a pretty sour look as he finished his telegram and sent for a hired hand to ride it into Blessing, seven miles away. I said, "Norris, let's don't make a big fuss about this. That land ain't even crossed my mind in at least a couple of years. Likely we got a few Mexican families squatting down there and trying to scratch out a few acres of corn."

Norris gave me his businessman's look. He said, "It's our land, Justa. And if we allow anyone to squat on it for long enough or put up a fence they can lay claim. That's the law. My job is to see that we protect what we have, not give it away."

I sipped at my whiskey and studied Norris. In his town clothes he didn't look very impressive. He'd inherited more from our mother than from Dad so he was not as wide-shouldered and slim-hipped as Ben and me. But I knew him to be a good, strong, dependable man in any kind of fight. Of course he wasn't that good with a gun, but then Ben and I weren't all that good with books like he was. But I said, just to jolly him a bit, "Norris, I do believe you are running to suet. I may have to put you out with Ben working the horse herd and work a little of that fat off you."

Naturally it got his goat. Norris had always envied Ben and me a little. I was just over six foot and weighed right around a hundred and ninety. I had inherited my daddy's big hands and big shoulders. Ben was almost a copy of me except he was about a size smaller. Norris said, "I weigh the same as I have for the last five years. If it's any of your business."

I said, as if I was being serious, "Must be them sack suits you wear. What they do, pad them around the middle?"

He said, "Why don't you just go to hell."

After he'd stomped out of the room I got the bottle of whiskey and an extra glass and went down to Dad's room. It had been one of his bad days and held taken to bed right after lunch. Strictly speaking he wasn't supposed to have no whiskey, but I watered him down a shot every now and then and it didn't seem to do him no harm.

He was sitting up when I came in the room. I took a moment to fix him a little drink, using some water out of his pitcher, then handed him the glass and sat down in the easy chair by the bed. I told him what Norris had reported and asked what he thought.

He took a sip of his drink and shook his head. "Beats all I ever heard," he said. "I took that land in trade for a bad debt some fifteen, twenty years ago. I reckon I'd of been money ahead if I'd of hung on to the bad debt. That land won't even raise weeds, well as I remember, and Noah was in on the last rain that fell on the place."

We had considerable amounts of land spotted around the state as a result of this kind of trade or that. It was Norris's business to keep up with their management. I was just bringing this to Dad's attention more out of boredom and impatience for my wedding day to arrive than anything else.

I said, "Well, it's a mystery to me. How you feeling?"

He half smiled. "Old." Then he looked into his glass.

"And I never liked watered whiskey. Pour me a dollop of the straight stuff in here."

I said, "Now, Howard. You know—"

He cut me off. "If I wanted somebody to argue with I'd send for Buttercup. Now do like I told you."

I did, but I felt guilty about it. He took the slug of whiskey down in one pull. Then he leaned his head back on the pillow and said, "Aaaaah. I don't give a damn what that horse doctor says, ain't nothing makes a man feel as good inside as a shot of the best."

I felt sorry for him laying there. He'd always led just the kind of life he wanted—going where he wanted, doing what he wanted, having what he set out to get. And now he was reduced to being a semi-invalid. But one thing that showed the strength that was still in him was that you *never* heard him complain. He said, "How's the cattle?"

I said, "They're doing all right, but I tell you we could do with a little of Noah's flood right now. All this heat and no rain is curing the grass off way ahead of time. If it doesn't let up we'll be feeding hay by late September, early October. And that will play hell on our supply. Could be we won't have enough to last through the winter. Norris thinks we ought to sell off five hundred head or so, but the market is doing poorly right now. I'd rather chance the weather than take a sure beating by selling off."

He sort of shrugged and closed his eyes. The whiskey was relaxing him. He said, "You're the boss."

"Yeah," I said. "Damn my luck."

I wandered out of the back of the house. Even though it was nearing seven o'clock of the evening it was still good and hot. Off in the distance, about a half a mile away, I could see the outline of the house I was building for Nora and myself. It was going to be a close thing to get it finished by our wedding day. Not having any riders to spare for the project, I'd imported a building contractor from Galveston, sixty miles away. He'd arrived with a half a dozen Mexican laborers and a few skilled masons and they'd set up a little tent city around the place. The contractor had gone back to Galveston to fetch more materials, leaving his Mexicans behind. I walked along idly, helping he wouldn't forget that the job wasn't done. He had some of my money, but not near what he'd get when he finished the job.

Just then Ray Hays came hurrying across the back lot toward me. Ray was kind of a special case for me. The only problem with that was that he knew it and wasn't a bit above taking advantage of the situation. Once, a few years past, he'd saved my life by going against an evil man that he was working for at the time, an evil man who meant to have my life. In gratitude I'd given Ray a good job at the Half-Moon, letting him work directly under Ben, who was responsible for the horse herd. He was a good, steady man and a good man with a gun. He was also fair company. When he wasn't talking.

He came churning up to me, mopping his brow. He said, "Lordy, boss, it is—"

I said, "Hays, if you say it's hot I'm going to knock you down."

He gave me a look that was a mixture of astonishment and hurt. He said, "Why, whatever for?"

I said, "*Everybody* knows it's hot. Does every son of a bitch you run into have to make mention of the fact?"

His brow furrowed. "Well, I never thought of it that way. I 'spect you are right. Goin' down to look at yore house?"

I shook my head. "No. It makes me nervous to see how far they've got to go. I can't see any way it'll be ready on time."

He said, "Miss Nora ain't gonna like that."

I gave him a look. "I guess you felt forced to say that."

He looked down. "Well, maybe she won't mind."

I said, grimly, "The hell she won't. She'll think I did it a-purpose."

"Aw, she wouldn't."

"Naturally you know so much about it, Hays. Why don't you tell me a few other things about her."

"I was jest tryin' to lift yore spirits, boss."

I said, "You keep trying to lift my spirits and I'll put you on the haying crew."

He looked horrified. No real cowhand wanted any work he couldn't do from the back of his horse. Haying was a hot, hard, sweaty job done either afoot or from a wagon seat. We generally brought in contract Mexican labor to handle ours. But I'd been known in the past to discipline a cowhand by giving him a few days on the hay gang. Hays said, "Boss, now I never meant nothin'. I swear. You know me, my mouth gets to runnin' sometimes. I swear I'm gonna watch it."

I smiled. Hays always made me smile. He was so easily buffaloed. He had it soft at the Half-Moon and he knew it and didn't want to take any chances on losing a good thing.

I lit up a cigarillo and watched dusk settle in over the coastal plains. It wasn't but three miles to Matagorda Bay and it was quiet enough I felt like I could almost hear the waves breaking on the shore. Somewhere in the distance a mama cow bawled for her calf. The spring crop were near about weaned by now, but there were still a few mamas that wouldn't cut the apron strings. I stood there reflecting on how peaceful things had been of late. It suited me just fine. All I wanted was to get my house finished, marry Nora and never handle another gun so long as I lived.

The peace and quiet were short-lived. Within twenty-four hours we'd had a return telegram from Jack Cole. It said:

YOUR LAND OCCUPIED BY TEN TO TWELVE MEN STOP CAN'T BE SURE WHAT THEY'RE DOING BECAUSE THEY RUN STRANGERS OFF STOP APPEAR TO HAVE A GOOD MANY CATTLE GATHERED STOP APPEAR TO BE FENCING STOP ALL I KNOW STOP

I read the telegram twice and then I said, "Why this is crazy as hell! That land wouldn't support fifty head of cattle."

We were all gathered in the big office. Even Dad was

there, sitting in his rocking chair. I looked up at him. "What do you make of this, Howard?"

He shook his big, old head of white hair. "Beats the hell out of me, Justa. I can't figure it."

Ben said, "Well, I don't see where it has to be figured. I'll take five men and go down there and run them off. I don't care what they're doing. They ain't got no business on our land."

I said, "Take it easy, Ben. Aside from the fact you don't need to be getting into any more fights this year, I can't spare you or five men. The way this grass is drying up we've got to keep drifting those cattle."

Norris said, "No, Ben is right. We can't have such affairs going on with our property. But we'll handle it within the law. I'll simply take the train down there, hire a good lawyer and have the matter settled by the sheriff. Shouldn't take but a few days."

Well, there wasn't much I could say to that. We couldn't very well let people take advantage of us, but I still hated to be without Norris's services even for a few days. On matters other than the ranch he was the expert, and it didn't seem like there was a day went by that some financial question didn't come up that only he could answer. I said, "Are you sure you can spare yourself for a few days?"

He thought for a moment and then nodded. "I don't see why not. I've just moved most of our available cash into short-term municipal bonds in Galveston. The market is looking all right and everything appears fine at the bank. I can't think of anything that might come up."

I said, "All right. But you just keep this in mind. You are not a gun hand. You are not a fighter. I do not want you going anywhere near those people, whoever they are. You do it legal and let the sheriff handle the eviction. Is that understood?"

He kind of swelled up, resenting the implication that he couldn't handle himself. The biggest trouble I'd had through the years when trouble had come up had been keeping Norris out of it. Why he couldn't just be content to be a wagon load of brains was more than I could understand. He said, "Didn't you just hear me say I intended to go through a lawyer and the sheriff? Didn't I just say that?"

I said, "I wanted to be sure you heard yourself."

He said, "Nothing wrong with my hearing. Nor my approach to this matter. You seem to constantly be taken with the idea that I'm always looking for a fight. I think you've got the wrong brother. I use logic."

"Yeah?" I said. "You remember when that guy kicked you in the balls when they were holding guns on us? And then we chased them twenty miles and finally caught them?"

He looked away. "That has nothing to do with this."

"Yeah?" I said, enjoying myself. "And here's this guy, shot all to hell. And what was it you insisted on doing?"

Ben laughed, but Norris wouldn't say anything.

I said, "Didn't you insist on us standing him up so you could kick him in the balls? Didn't you?"

He sort of growled, "Oh, go to hell."

I said, "I just want to know where the logic was in that."

He said, "Right is right. I was simply paying him back in kind. It was the only thing his kind could understand."

I said, "That's my point. You just don't go down there and go to paying back a bunch of rough hombres in kind. Or any other currency for that matter."

That made him look over at Dad. He said, "Dad, will you make him quit treating me like I was ten years old? He does it on purpose."

But he'd appealed to the wrong man. Dad just threw his hands in the air and said, "Don't come to me with your troubles. I'm just a boarder around here. You get your orders from Justa. You know that."

Of course he didn't like that. Norris had always been a strong hand for the right and wrong of a matter. In fact, he may have been one of the most stubborn men I'd ever met. But he didn't say anything, just gave me a look and muttered something about hoping a mess came up at the bank while he was gone and then see how much boss I was.

But he didn't mean nothing by it. Like most families, we fought amongst ourselves and, like most families, God help the outsider who tried to interfere with one of us.

WESTERNS!

at least a savings of $3.00 each month below the publishers price. Second, there is never any shipping, handling or other hidden charges—Free home delivery. What's more there is no minimum number of books you must buy, you may return any selection for full credit and you can cancel your subscription at any time. A TRUE VALUE!

Mail the coupon below

To start your subscription and receive 2 FREE WESTERNS, fill out the coupon below and mail it today. We'll send your first shipment which includes 2 FREE BOOKS as soon as we receive it.